W9-BQM-107

Dear Reader,

Do you like dogs? I am so not a dog person that I empathized with one of our characters while writing this book. I hope you dog lovers will forgive me. The story grew on me, and when my husband read the finished product, he said it sounded as though I was beginning to like dogs. Was I ready for a puppy? I assured him I was not, though I admit the photo my editor sent me of his schnoodle pup for inspiration was downright adorable.

The Miracles of Marble Cove stories always seem to hit a personal spot. One other thing that resonated with me in this story was the Maine winter. I've been through more than fifty of those, and I understand how trying they can be. As you read this story, I hope you're someplace warm and comfortable and don't have to worry about how you'll get out of your driveway in the morning.

In this book, all of the friends are growing as they face difficult situations. My hope is that you'll learn what they have—when times get tough, the Lord is always there to help you. Of course, a little support from friends and family never hurts!

Blessings,
Susan Page Davis

MIRACLES *of*
MARBLE COVE

FRIENDS AND FAMILY

SUSAN PAGE DAVIS

Guideposts
New York

Published by Guideposts
110 William Street
New York, NY 10038
Guideposts.org

Acknowledgments

Every attempt has been made to credit the sources of copyrighted material used in this book. If any such acknowledgment has been inadvertently omitted or miscredited, receipt of such information would be appreciated.

"Grandma Bauer's Depression-Era Cake" and "From the Guideposts Archive" originally appeared in *Guideposts* magazine. Copyright © 2009 and 1986, respectively, by Guideposts. All rights reserved.

Cover and interior design and photography by Müllerhaus
Images by Shutterstock and Masterfile
Typeset by Aptara, Inc.

Printed and bound in the United States of America
10 9 8 7 6 5 4

CHAPTER ONE

Diane Spencer stood at the window of her cottage, looking out at the pristine snow blanketing her yard. For the past few months, the winter weather on the Maine coast had added to the burden of her illness, making it more difficult to get around to appointments and discouraging her from doing much outside. But now she was feeling better— so much better that the sun sparkling on the snow called up a childlike joy inside her.

Across Newport Avenue, her neighbor Shelley was playing on her lawn with her toddler. The sight gave Diane the nudge she needed. She turned around and looked at her dog, who sat eyeing her, waiting for a cue.

"Want to go for a walk, Rocky?"

He yipped and leaped up, wagging his tail.

Diane laughed and headed for the coat closet. "Let me get rigged up." She exchanged her slippers for faux fur-lined boots and put on a warm, powder-blue jacket. Over her short brown hair, just growing out to presentable length, she pulled a red-and-white hat. She looped the matching scarf around her neck. Gloves next, and then she reached for Rocky's leash.

"Okay, boy! Let's go!"

He lunged happily to her side. Diane opened the door and squinted for a moment against the glare of the sun. The new snowfall had added about two inches to what had already accumulated—about six inches deep on the lawn. The walkway and drive were navigable, and Diane plunged into it, savoring the crunch of the new snow packing beneath her boots.

She let Rocky race around the yard, sending up little clouds of flakes that glittered like pixie dust. He poked his nose into a drift and sniffed at snow-covered shrubs.

After a couple of minutes, Diane called to him. He lumbered to her side and let her clip the leash to his collar before they crossed the street. This time of year, hardly any traffic came down Newport Avenue.

Shelley pushed a large snowball across her lawn, with two-year-old Emma lurching along in her wake.

"Hey," Diane called, "are you building a snowman?"

Shelley looked over at her and laughed. "Trying. Emma's no help. She's just playing around. I really miss Aiden on days like this."

"I'll bet," Diane said. "I could help."

"Great," Shelley said.

Diane let Rocky loose in the Bauers' fenced yard and crouched down next to Emma. "Hi! Do you like the snow?"

"I think she's getting a little tired of it," Shelley said. "She'll be much happier when it's warm and we can play on the beach more."

"Won't we all?" Diane scooped up a handful of snow. "Look, Emma. Do you know how to make a snowball?"

"'No-ball," Emma said.

Diane laughed. "That's right." She looked over at Shelley. "Okay, what do you want me to do?"

"This is his tummy," Shelley said. "Can you roll him a head the right size?"

"I think I can handle that." Diane set to work, and a few minutes later, the stubby shape of a snowman graced the Bauers' lawn. Emma staggered over to him and patted the base, looking up at her mother for approval.

"That's right," Shelley said. "Make him nice and smooth."

"What do you use for the face?" Diane asked.

"I usually use pebbles for the eyes," Shelley said.

"What, no coal?"

"Afraid not. I do have carrots, though. We can use one for his nose."

Emma began to howl, and both women spun toward her. She was crouched down, with one hand exposed to the cold air, and Diane couldn't help smiling at her woeful face.

Shelley laughed and waded through the snow to the little girl. "What happened, Emma? Looks like you lost your mitten."

Emma sobbed and held up her pudgy little hand. "'No!"

"Yeah, snow. Cold, isn't it?" Shelley smiled at Diane. "I think someone's had enough, and it's about N-A-P time. Care for a cup of cocoa with me?"

"Sounds good. Oh, here's her mitten." Diane pulled the soggy pink mitten from the snow at Shelley's feet.

They trudged inside, with Rocky at Diane's heels. The Bauers' little dog Prize greeted him enthusiastically. After a moment the two calmed down, and Rocky lay down on the rug beside Prize.

Shelley took off Emma's boots and snowsuit and carried her off to her room. Diane took off her own outdoor gear and stepped into the kitchen. She'd been to Shelley's house often enough to know where the cups and hot chocolate mix were kept. By the time her hostess returned, she had two steaming mugs ready.

"Thanks, Diane!" Shelley went to the counter and picked up a rectangular plastic container. "Here are the rejects from yesterday's baking. Help yourself." She opened the box and set it on the table.

Diane gazed at an array of slightly imperfect cookies, Danish, and cream puffs.

"Oh my. You know you tempt me terribly every time I come here."

"Well, you can stand it right now," Shelley said. "I know you lost weight during your weekly treatments. I hope you can get a little stronger soon. Although you did pretty well with the snowman."

"I'm doing much better, thanks. Now that my treatments are down to twice a month, I'm starting to enjoy food again. In fact, that cherry Danish right there is calling my name." Diane reached for the pastry and slid it onto her napkin. "How are *you* doing? Have you recovered from the holiday rush?"

Shelley chuckled. "I'm into the next holiday rush already. I'm making Valentine cookies again. Last year they were a big hit, so I advertised them again. I've already got almost fifty orders, so you know what I'll be making for the next two weeks."

Diane laughed. "Terrific. Have you got all your boxes and everything ready?"

"Yeah, I learned a lot last year. I think it will go more smoothly this time. And it was a big moneymaker. I spent most of the morning working on those, after I'd done the usual pastries for the Cove and the B and Bs, but Emma was tired of not getting my attention. She'll sleep now, though." Shelley looked at Diane critically. "Are you sure you're all right?"

"I'm fine."

"I didn't mean to insult you, but you look tired."

Diane grimaced. "Sorry. I do feel better." After another sip of cocoa, she said, "You know what I keep thinking about?"

Shelley shook her head, eyeing her anxiously.

"The old Thorpe house."

"Oh, that." Shelley laughed. "I should have known. But the people who own it now are out of state. We can't do anything about it until they come back for the summer, can we?"

"Well, I don't know," Diane said. "The neighbor mentioned that someone is taking care of the house for them. Raking the snow off the roof and shoveling sidewalks—that sort of thing. If we can find out who it is, maybe he can tell us a little about the house."

"It would be nice to learn something about it, especially if it helped us find out what happened to Elias Thorpe." Shelley's eyebrows drew together as she absently munched a cookie. "How do you suppose he could have had such a nice big house on his salary?"

"Maybe he made good investments," Diane said. "We don't know how much he got paid as stationmaster."

"Well, I can't imagine he got rich running that little railroad depot," Shelley insisted. "It makes me wonder how he could have lived like he did. Maybe he was involved in something shady on the side."

Diane laughed. "What makes you think that?"

"I don't know. There must have been opportunities for him to make some extra money. Maybe people bribed him to haul things he wasn't supposed to."

"Wow, you're full of wild theories today."

Shelley laughed. "Sorry. I just know there's something fishy about that guy."

"You may be right," Diane said. "But all we really know is that he dropped out of sight the day the last train left the Marble Cove station. There's no law against moving away when your job ends."

"But he didn't just move away. He disappeared into thin air!"

"Okay, I'll give you that. His disappearance does look suspicious. I guess that's why I keep hoping we can find another clue soon."

"Well, you just take care of yourself," Shelley said. "I'm sure when spring comes, we'll be right back in the thick of it."

"Something tells me we won't have to wait that long," Diane said with a chuckle.

* * *

Beverly spent three hours at her desk in the mayor's office. The next council meeting was eight days away, but she wanted to be sure she was prepared. A big part of that involved staying on top of local issues. She did a lot of reading on taxes and tourism, as well as small-business concerns and environmental topics. The budget for the next fiscal year also needed consideration. Compiling it wasn't the mayor's job, but she intended to know the last budget inside out and be ready to question any proposed expenses that the town couldn't afford.

Beverly excelled at financial planning and budgets, having formerly served as a budget analyst for the Maine House of Representatives. The town's allotments were tiny by comparison, but every bit as important to the residents of Marble Cove.

Would the town treasurer, Lionel Riley, who was in charge of this task, resent Beverly's input? She hoped not, but it wouldn't stop her from taking a hard look at the numbers.

As she delved into the budget, she was sure the town could save a few dollars here and there. On the other hand, judicious spending on promotion could make a big difference in attracting tourists for the summer season, which would feed the local economy. Some of the residents—especially older people who had lived in the little village all their lives—couldn't see the point of advertising. They believed that the charming little town would speak for itself.

A lot of people did visit Marble Cove in summer, and the beach and festivities contributed to that. But Beverly believed in publicity, and this town had barely tapped the possibilities.

She stood and stretched. Father and Mrs. Peabody would expect her home for lunch. Before leaving the room, she paused at the window and admired the view of Main Street.

The inside of the office was less to her liking. She needed to redo the walls, and soon. Beverly found Evelyn Waters' choice of décor jarring. The former mayor had selected lavender-and-white-striped wallpaper, with a border of cherubs and nosegays of violets. The lace curtains might be all right, but Beverly preferred something more practical—something businesslike. She would feel much more professional bringing people up here for interviews and business conversations if the room looked more like an office, not a Victorian parlor.

Beverly's head spun with facts and figures about town business, and she was ready to move on to something more imaginative. She decided to go downstairs and talk to Angela in person. If she wasn't too busy, she might be able to help her learn more about the old Elias Thorpe house.

She gathered the materials she wanted to take home with her and put the files in her soft leather briefcase. From the antique coat tree, she took her warm, charcoal wool coat and floppy red hat. She carried them over her arm and took her purse from the desk drawer and headed downstairs.

"Hello," Angela said with a bright smile as Beverly entered the reception room. "How can I help you?"

"Hi. I mentioned to you a few days ago that I'm interested in the house that Elias Thorpe owned once."

"Oh, right. We looked it up in the tax records and got those blueprints."

"Yes, and that was great. I'm wondering now about the current owners, Bartholomew and Mildred Inglewood. Do you know who might be looking out for the house while they're away—you know, checking for security, or raking the snow off the roof after a bad storm, that sort of thing?"

"*Hmm.*" Angela brushed her short hair back off her forehead. "There's a guy who checks on quite a few of the summer cottages for people…uh, Willard Rockwell, and I'm almost sure he told me once he was looking after their house too."

As she spoke, a man came into the room pulling out his wallet.

"That's a big help, Angela. Thanks," Beverly said as Angela turned her attention to the customer. "I'll see you soon."

⋏ ⋏ ⋏

When she walked in the front door of the house Beverly now shared with her father, the aroma coming from the kitchen indicated they were in for a delicious lunch of meatloaf and herbed mashed potatoes.

Unbuttoning her coat, she stepped into the doorway. "Mrs. Peabody, it smells heavenly in here."

The older woman turned, wiping her hands on the skirt of her bib apron.

"Well, thank you. I wondered if you'd get home on time today."

Beverly smiled. She had gotten used to Mrs. Peabody's clipped manner and had become quite fond of her.

"I'm home for the rest of the day," Beverly told her.

Mrs. Peabody grunted. "I'm putting lunch on the table in five minutes."

"I'll be ready." Beverly hung her coat in the hall closet and tucked her hat and gloves into pockets of the organizer inside the door. She glanced into the living room, which was vacant, and moved on to her father's library.

"Well, hi." He lowered the book he had been reading and smiled at her. His gray eyes looked large through the thick lenses of his glasses. "How's it going? Are you making Marble Cove a better place?"

She laughed. "I hope so."

Mrs. Peabody called them to lunch and the two made their way to the table.

"Do you know a Willard Rockwell here in town?" Beverly asked her father as they settled into their chairs.

"I know who he is, but I wouldn't say I know him personally. He's a fisherman."

"He takes care of people's cottages in the winter."

"That makes sense."

"Well, the old Elias Thorpe house is one of the properties he watches," Beverly noted.

"Are you thinking of getting in touch with Mr. Rockwell?" her father asked.

"Why not?" Beverly responded. "With any luck, he just might be able to help us save the old train depot and figure out what happened to Elias Thorpe all those years ago."

CHAPTER TWO

Shelley carefully balanced two boxes containing pastries and cookies while she nudged the car door shut for her Tuesday morning delivery to the Cove.

"Emma, stay with Mama."

Her little girl obediently toddled along beside her to the back door of the coffee shop. As Shelley struggled to find the door handle without tipping her boxes, Brenna McTavish appeared inside and smiled as she pushed the door open.

"Hi! Let me take those."

"Thanks," Shelley said, sliding the boxes into Brenna's hands. "There's more in the car. Can Emma stay inside while I get them?"

"Of course. Come on in, sweetie," Brenna said to Emma. The little girl walked into the kitchen behind Brenna.

Emma was familiar enough with the Cove and Brenna that she wouldn't fuss while Shelley made the short return trip to her car. The early-morning deliveries were easier now that Emma was walking well and Aiden was off to preschool every weekday.

Shelley soon had all of the fresh pastries inside. Brenna gave her two clean trays to take home and reuse. Shelley was just about to herd Emma out the door when the shop's owner, Rusty Garrison, came in from the dining area.

"Shelley! Just the gal I want to see."

"Hi, Rusty. How's it going?"

"Business is good. That's what I want to talk to you about. Have you thought any more about taking over this place when I retire?"

"Some. Not a lot, I admit. But the idea is exciting. I've always dreamed of having my own bakery." Shelley glanced toward Brenna, but the young woman was heading out to the counter area with a large container of ground coffee.

"Well, give it some serious thought." Rusty ran a hand over his silver-flecked red hair. "I'm thinking I'd like to retire in the spring."

"This spring?" Shelley's voice croaked, and Emma toddled over and grabbed her leg. Shelley stooped and lifted her with one arm. "It's okay, sweetie." She looked back at Rusty. "That's kind of soon, isn't it? I thought you were going to keep working for two or three more years."

"I was thinking of sticking it out another year or two, but you know, Wendy and I would really like to have the freedom to get away and do the things we've always wanted to do. The longer I wait, the less time we have to do them." Rusty nodded firmly. "I'd like to retire before all the tourists come in June and it gets busy again. I'm ready."

"Wow." Shelley stood for a moment, stunned, as Emma patted her hair. "Rusty, I don't know what to say. I've thought about it a little, and I discussed it some with Dan. But we hadn't really come to a decision about it. I was thinking it was…you know, in the future."

"Yeah, well, it was, but Wendy and I would like to make that future a little more immediate is all. And the numbers look good right now, so I think it's time."

"That's great," Shelley said. "Uh…you know, we might not be ready for that. The family, I mean. What would you do if I decided I couldn't take it on?"

Rusty shrugged. "Brenna's not in a position to do it. I'd probably advertise the place and try to sell it."

Shelley nodded. "Okay. I'll definitely consider it, and I'll try to get back to you soon. Dan's working out of town a lot right now, though. I'm not sure when we'll be able to sit down and hash it over."

"Well, when you can," Rusty said.

Emma was getting heavy, and Shelley slid her to the floor. "Come on, sweetie. You can walk." She shifted the trays under her arm. "Thanks, Rusty. I do appreciate your confidence in me." She took Emma out to the car and buckled her into her seat, her mind whirling with possibilities. Did she really want to manage the Cove full-time? It would mean a steady income, but was she ready to manage a busy coffee shop and run her bakery business from there? And was it the right course for the family?

★ ★ ★

Diane came out of the post office and unhooked Rocky's leash from the leg of a nearby bench. She'd left him for just a minute while she went inside to mail a signed copy of her first novel to a reviewer.

Rocky lifted his face to hers and licked her cheek as she bent over him.

"Oh, you want to get kissy?" Diane asked with a laugh. "It's a little cold out for that." She rubbed her cheek dry with the back of her glove. "Come on, let's go home."

A car pulled into a parking space right in front of them, and she smiled at the driver, Dr. Leo Spangler, her friend and Rocky's vet.

"Hi, Diane," Leo said cheerfully as he climbed out of the car. "Hey, Rocky! Looking good, boy!" He bent to pat the dog's silky head. In his hand was a sheaf of envelopes. "I ran out of stamps, so I had to stop at the post office on my way to the clinic."

"I just came from there," Diane said. "Beautiful day, if you like sunny and forty degrees."

"I do," Leo said. "In fact, I was thinking how nice it would be to take a day and go over to Sugarloaf for some skiing." He eyed her keenly. "Do you ski?"

"I used to, but it's been a while," Diane said. "Eric and I used to go now and then. But I'm way out of practice, and I honestly don't think I'd be up to it now. Although I could probably handle hot chocolate by the fireplace in the lodge."

Leo's expression changed to one of concern. "How are you feeling these days?"

"Not bad. I still have bad days when I'm a little wobbly, but I'm trying to get out more and get some sun when I can, to regain a little muscle tone."

He nodded gravely. "I'm glad you're doing better. I was thinking about calling you and asking…well, do you have plans for Valentine's Day?"

Diane chuckled. "After what happened last year? Are you sure you would want to spend it with me?"

Leo laughed sheepishly. "I don't know about you, but I thought it ended up being a fun evening. Not what I'd expected—washing dishes at the Landmark and waiting on tables, but I'm willing to risk it again. How about it?"

"Can I think about it?" The casual meeting had suddenly taken on an edge of tension. Diane didn't want to commit to a date and regret it later. On the other hand, she didn't want to refuse and then feel depressed about it, wondering if she had hurt Leo's feelings. He was a good friend. She just wasn't sure she wanted to change what they had now to something more romantic, and if two people made a regular thing of a Valentine's dinner date, wouldn't everyone else assume they were a true couple? No, she wasn't ready to project that image, to Leo or to other people.

"Sure," he said easily, but some of the eagerness had gone out of his blue eyes. "Want to call me when you've thought it over?"

"Okay." Diane smiled. "Well, Rocky and I had better get moving. Nice to see you, Leo."

"Same here." He headed for the post office, and Diane lifted the leash, her signal to Rocky that she was ready to walk.

She was in no hurry to go home. The sun shone bright, and the snowbanks left by the plow were settling and shrinking. They were near Margaret Hoskins' gallery, so Diane guided Rocky toward her friend's business.

Margaret was behind the counter when they entered. She threw Diane a big smile and finished checking out a customer. Diane took Rocky to Margaret's office in the back.

"Lie down, boy," she told him. When he obeyed, she stroked his head. "Good boy. Stay."

When she went back into the front room, Margaret's customer had left.

"Diane, it's so good to see you." Margaret came toward her smiling. "Can you have a cup of coffee with me? I'm ready for a break."

"I'd love to."

Both were soon seated in the back room with steaming mugs of coffee and one of Shelley's oatmeal-raisin cookies.

"It's a beautiful day," Margaret said. "People are getting out and about. I had quite a flurry of business earlier."

"It's lovely," Diane agreed. "I saw several people I know on the way here, and I ran into Leo outside the post office. I'll understand if you need to leave me suddenly to tend to customers."

Margaret zoomed in on one thing in her comments. "Leo, huh? He's such a nice guy."

"Yes." Diane felt her cheeks warm. It was silly, really. She wasn't a schoolgirl, to blush over the mention of a man's name. And it wasn't as if she was romantically involved with the veterinarian. "Can I ask you something?"

"Sure," Margaret said.

Diane hesitated. "Well, see, he asked me out. For Valentine's Day."

"What did you tell him?"

"I said I'd think about it. I didn't know what to say, really. I like him, but I don't want to send too strong a signal. He's been very supportive during this last round of cancer treatments, and helpful as well. And we've had some movie nights together, and that was fun. I just…"

"You don't want him to think you're in love with him."

Diane let out a little sigh. "That's right. Am I sending him the wrong signal? He's sweet, and I'm not saying I could never love him. But I'm not sure that will ever happen, and I don't want him making assumptions." She spread her hands in helplessness. "I don't think I'm ready for romance, with Leo or anyone else. I still don't feel good some days. I don't want to be dependent on somebody and have him think I'm looking at him as husband material."

Margaret nodded. "And you want to make sure he knows the difference."

"Well…yes." Diane sipped her coffee. "Holidays are hard, you know?"

"Yes, they are. And you did spend some time with Leo at Thanksgiving and Christmas."

"Exactly. Is he starting to expect that we'll spend every holiday together?"

"You know," Margaret said, "you're used to being a caregiver. Maybe that's what makes it so hard for you to accept Leo's friendship right now."

Diane looked at her in surprise. "Do you think so?"

"I know so. You're very nurturing—always helping other people. You've helped me, and Shelley and Dan, and Beverly, Mr. Wheeland, your summer neighbors, your children—I could go on and on. Even in your lowest moments, you reach out to others. Look at your blog!"

Diane sat back, confused. "Oh, that. I didn't start that intending it to be a ministry."

"I know. But it's become one, hasn't it? People write comments telling how much your posts mean to them, and you answer them and let them tell you their stories. You listen. You care about them."

"I guess that's true." Diane smiled, thinking of all the wonderful online relationships she'd formed since her cancer had returned. "I feel as if God has used my experience to comfort a few people."

"More than a few, my dear. Oops—" As the bell over the gallery's front door rang, Margaret leaned forward and craned her neck to see out into the other room. "Excuse me. I may or may not be back soon."

Diane sat back with a sigh. She should probably go on home, but she would like to continue the discussion with Margaret. She saw the truth of what her friend had said—that she was more comfortable in the role of caregiver than she was receiving help from others. But she wasn't sure how that related to her ambivalence toward Leo. His interest in her couldn't be compared to a ministry, could it? To her, his concern seemed very personal, which made her hesitate to encourage him. Their friendship had grown into a comfortable relationship. But did Leo want more than she could give at this point in her life?

Maybe she needed time to think it all through on her own. She sipped her coffee and finished off the chewy oatmeal cookie, thankful that such simple things gave her pleasure. As she did several times a day, she silently thanked God for letting her body, with help from the medical team that served her, beat the cancer.

Margaret returned, apologetic. "Just a browser. Now, where were we?"

"Actually, I wanted to speak to you about Elias Thorpe. I feel like we've hit a wall. But I want to find out as much as we can about him and the train station."

"So do I," Margaret said. "I'm not sure how much we can do this winter."

Diane chatted with her a few more minutes, just as happy to put the topic of Leo aside. She would think over his invitation and the observations Margaret had made again when she was alone.

"I think Beverly was going to try to find out more about the people who own his old house now," she said. "Maybe she'll turn up a lead we can follow."

"That would be fun," Margaret said.

Rocky whined and looked up at Diane with huge brown eyes.

She chuckled. "Someone wants to continue our walk, and you need to get back to work, I'm sure." She stood and zipped her jacket. As she pulled on her gloves, the bell rang.

"There's another customer," Margaret said. "I'm awfully glad you came by."

"So am I." With a big smile, Diane picked up the end of Rocky's leash. "Up, boy."

He leaped to his feet and all but pulled her to the door.

"I'll see you again soon," Diane called as they headed out into the winter dazzle of Main Street.

★ ★ ★

Beverly was just a little nervous on Wednesday morning. Jeff was coming to take her and her father to lunch. She had needed several months of small doses to become comfortable with Jeff. Seeing him again would be exciting enough, but today's outing would probably include running into other people she knew at the restaurant. Now that she was mayor, people tended to approach her anyplace, anytime. Usually they were nice about it, but now and then someone tried to buttonhole her and pitch his own ideas on how the town should be run.

As she checked her silhouette in the full-length mirror in her room—black slacks, snowy-white blouse, and tweed blazer—she heard his SUV drive in. She grabbed her phone and purse and hurried down the stairs to let him in.

Jeff was mounting the front steps when she opened the front door, and his face lit up.

"Hey! You look great."

"Thanks." She tipped her face up to his. "So do you."

Jeff kissed her and then stepped back, holding out a small bouquet in a cellophane wrap. "I thought maybe you were ready for some color. February gets pretty dull."

Her heart melted. Jeff, with his artist's eye, would think of that. She took the bunch of deep pink tulips.

"Thank you—and you're right. I won't be sorry when the snow goes and the daffodils start blooming again."

He followed her into the kitchen. Beverly had told Mrs. Peabody she needn't come today, and the older lady had seemed happy to have a day off. The next thing Beverly heard was that Mrs. Peabody's granddaughter was whisking her off to Augusta for the day.

She took down a cut-glass vase that had belonged to her mother and arranged the tulips.

"Father's ready to go," she said, carrying the vase to the sink. "He's in the library, so I'll tell him you're here."

"I can tell him," Jeff offered. "Do you think he'd rather go to Captain Calhoun's or the Landmark?"

"Either one is fine." She reached for the faucet handle.

"Oh, before I forget," Jeff said.

She paused, looking up into his face. Her heart fluttered. How did she end up with this paragon of a man?

"I want to make sure you're saving Valentine's Day for me."

She beamed. "Of course! I wouldn't spend it with anyone else. I wasn't sure you'd be in town though."

"Well, I have to leave tomorrow for a run to Vermont, but I'll be back next week. Let's plan on dinner."

"All right. And would you be able to come early enough to go and see Reverend Locke? We need to talk to him about the church. For the wedding, you know." Her cheeks felt warm, and she hated that. What was so embarrassing about planning a wedding with her fiancé?

"Sure," Jeff said. "I could come around five, I think. Would that be all right?"

"I'll call him and see if he can see us. Just a brief visit. I think we should see him face to face, in case he has any questions about the ceremony."

"Sounds good. I'll go tell your dad we're ready to go."

Beverly smiled and watched him go. She certainly had found a wonderful man.

She placed the vase of flowers on the dining room table. Jeff and her father came down the hallway together, talking easily about Jeff's recent trip. While she would never be so foolish as to think nothing could ever upset the pleasant rhythm of her life, she was starting to believe that she and Jeff had a wonderful future in store.

★ ★ ★

Allan arrived at the Shearwater Gallery at quarter to three. Margaret had already ducked into the restroom and changed into a long T-shirt and soft knit pants—one of the outfits she wore for her tai chi classes at the community center. In the office, she put on her winter jacket and hat.

"Thanks, honey," she said as she scooped up her keys and wallet. "I'll be back in an hour and a half."

"Take your time." Allan kissed her, just as the doorbell rang, announcing a new customer. "Get out while you can," he said with a smile.

Margaret slipped out the back door. The temperature was slightly above freezing, and water dripped from the eaves of all the buildings along Main Street. Icicles that had formed overnight loosened and fell into the snow below.

She walked briskly to her car and made the short drive to the community center. As she entered, Margaret nodded to the receptionist. Walking down a long hallway, she could hear the instructor of a more vigorous exercise class calling out instructions to the students. She was glad she'd found the gentler tai chi group.

Allan was a dear to watch the gallery a couple of times a week so she could go to the class. Since both of them had experienced wakeup calls regarding their health, they had both become more aware of their need to keep their bodies in shape. Tai chi was Margaret's answer, and they'd both started an evening ballroom dancing class.

A colorful poster on a bulletin board caught Margaret's eye just before she reached the room where her class was held. The center was hosting a Valentine's Day dinner for seniors. She didn't think she and Allan would want to attend, but seeing the bright poster embellished with red and pink hearts started her thinking about the coming holiday. She wanted to do something special for Allan, especially since his birthday was coming up too.

She took her place in the class and faced the smiling instructor.

"Hi, Margaret," said the woman next to her.

"Hello." Margaret smiled, but her thoughts were still on Valentine's Day. Allen usually brought her flowers, but they hadn't made a big deal of the holiday in the past. This year, she would make it extraspecial. The only question was, how?

* * *

Diane sat at her desk for an hour, working on her new devotional book. When her eyelids began to droop, she got up and stretched. She tired more quickly these days; there was no use denying it. A few months ago she'd been able to work on her writing for hours at a time, but now she needed more frequent breaks and even an occasional nap.

She walked to the kitchen, and Rocky got up and followed her. Diane took a moment to pat him and slip him a doggie treat. Next she filled a mug with water and put it in the microwave. Raspberry-flavored hot chocolate might wake her up a little.

While she waited for the water to heat, she thought about yesterday's encounter with Leo. Thinking about him sent her spirits plummeting, and she frowned, wondering why that was. Did the idea of letting any man into her life now depress her? Or was it just Leo?

It wasn't as if she wanted to be with some other man. Right now no one claimed that spot in her life. Now and then, loneliness did overtake her, but for the most part she enjoyed her solitude and the freedom it gave her.

The bell on the microwave rang, and she took out her mug. As she stirred the powdered beverage mix into the water, her phone rang.

"Hi, Mom!"

The caller was the one person who could send Diane's mood through the roof with two words.

"Jessica! It's great to hear your voice," Diane said.

"How are you doing?"

"Not too bad. It's been warm the past couple of days—or maybe I should say 'warmish.' Rocky and I have been getting out more."

"That's good. Just don't overdo it."

"No worries." Diane smiled at her daughter's concern. Jessica had a strong maternal streak. "How are the wedding plans going?"

"Well…"

Her hesitation sent up a red flag in Diane's mind.

"What? Is anything wrong?"

"I wouldn't say 'wrong.' I'm a little stressed, I guess. Every time I try to sit down with Martin and talk about the wedding and make some concrete plans, he sort of clams up."

"Really? That doesn't sound like Martin," Diane said. But then, how well did she really know the young man?

"It's probably nothing," Jessica said. "He's been real busy lately, and I know work is stressing him. He's had to train two new techs and do all his own work as well."

"That's not good. You know, men handle stress differently than we do."

"I keep telling myself everything's okay," Jessica admitted, "but sometimes everything seems off somehow."

Diane sat down at the kitchen table with her untouched mug of cocoa in front of her. "Are you two doing anything this weekend?"

"We're supposed to spend Saturday together."

"Maybe you should wait until then. After you do something fun and he's in a good mood, that might be a good time to bring up the wedding stuff."

"Oh, Mom."

"No, really," Diane said, stirring the hot chocolate slowly. "You two need to talk about this and get it out in the open. Tell him how you feel about his zoning out. But don't do it when either of you is upset. Look for a mellow moment."

"I'll try," Jessica said.

"Let me know how it goes."

"I will. And he's already made a reservation at a fancy restaurant for Valentine's Day."

"That sounds promising."

"Well, yeah, I guess. But it won't be any fun if the atmosphere is all tense." Jessica laughed. "So, Mom. Valentine's. Do *you* have any plans?"

"Me? No. Well, Leo Spangler asked me—"

"Leo? He's a great guy. What are you doing?"

"Nothing yet. I haven't given him an answer."

"Why not? You said you feel better."

"I do, but I'm not sure I'm ready for a relationship yet. Leo's a good friend, but I'm afraid he'll want it to go further than that."

"Aw, come on, Mom. We had a great time together over the holidays. Leo's a lot of fun, and very considerate."

"I'm still thinking about it," Diane said defensively.

"You do that."

Time to change the subject. "So, what do you want for your birthday?"

"Me?" Jessica asked. "I haven't even thought about it."

"Well, start thinking. It's less than three weeks away."

CHAPTER THREE

Shelley baked three dozen giant heart cookies on Thursday afternoon. With Hailey entertaining the children after she got home from school, Shelley was able to concentrate on her baking and accomplished more than usual. She sealed the fresh cookies in plastic bags and froze them to await decorating just before she shipped them. She was keeping up with her Valentine orders, which pleased her immensely.

As she rolled and rerolled the phyllo dough for the Danish pastries customers loved, she thought about Rusty Garrison's plea. What would her days be like if she managed the coffee shop on a daily basis? And would the increase in income be worth the time she would have to give up at home?

She slid two trays of pastries into the commercial oven and washed her hands. She'd have time for a quick glance at her e-mail. During her busy seasons, she found that she couldn't afford to ignore the Internet. Sure enough, three more cookie orders had come in. She noted them in her computer file for new orders, but also jotted them down in a notebook. If something drastic happened, she didn't want to lose her record of the orders. As one more step in assuring her efficiency, she backed up the computer file to an online storage site.

She could hear Hailey and Aiden talking eagerly as they played in Aiden's room. Sitting back in a rare moment of ease, Shelley glanced down through the list of cookie orders. Many came from repeat customers, but a lot of new people had ordered this year, and her sales were close to topping last year's Valentine orders.

The kitchen timer rang, and she hurried to take the Danish out of the oven. Perfect. The coffee drinkers at the Cove would be unable to resist these tomorrow morning. She wasn't so sure about how Dan would react when she brought up the subject of Rusty's retirement and his offer to her.

"Hey, Mom?"

She turned and smiled at Aiden, who stood in the doorway.

"What's up?" she asked.

"I think Emma's hungry."

Shelley laughed. This was one of Aiden's ways of saying he wanted a snack. "Well, tell Emma and Hailey to come to the table. I happen to have some broken cookies, and you all can have a little." She didn't tell him that the snack came from one of the giant heart cookies. He would want to eat the whole thing. She put pieces onto three small plates in appropriate portions for the children and carried them to the table. Hailey was lifting Emma onto her booster seat.

"Here you go." Shelley distributed the plates around the table. "Does everyone want milk?"

"Hey," Aiden said. "How come Hailey gets more than me?"

"Because she's bigger than you."

"Well, I'm a boy."

Hailey burst out in laughter.

"You get more than Emma," Shelley said, "and Hailey gets a little more than you. Not much, but a little."

Aiden frowned, but reached for one of his cookie pieces.

"Thanks for watching them," she said to her niece.

"They were good," Hailey said. "I'll have to do some homework after supper, though."

"No problem." Shelley would have only an hour or so of work left for this evening, and Dan would be home to help with the kids.

Now that Aiden was in preschool, she didn't spend a lot of time actually playing with him, and sometimes he acted up for attention. When they had finished their snacks, she would start potatoes cooking for supper and go spend a half hour with them.

★ ★ ★

Diane set out to call Leo several times before she finally put the call through on Thursday evening.

"Hi, Diane."

His voice sounded buoyant—expectant. She hated to bring him down, but she had to follow her heart on this.

Last year's double date with Jeff and Beverly had turned out okay despite her hesitation at that time as well. But now Jeff and Beverly were engaged, and Diane didn't want Leo to read anything into their relationship that she didn't intend. Better to tell him now, she reminded herself, than to let him go on hoping.

"Hi, Leo. I've been thinking about your invitation. Thanks so much for thinking of me, but…"

"But…," he prompted, matter-of-factly.

"But…I'm sorry. I just don't feel ready. I mean… Valentine's Day and all that. I know we both had fun last year, but…"

"Is it your illness?" he asked. "Because I could bring a movie over, and we could spend an evening in. Very low-key."

Diane hesitated. "I won't use my cancer as an excuse, although I admit I'm not back to my best yet. To be honest, I just don't feel ready to maintain a…a romantic relationship. And I feel as though that's where you'd like to take this. I'm really sorry, Leo."

"Hey, don't feel bad, Diane. Please. The last thing I want is to add stress to your life right now. I understand. We'll just put things on hold. Maybe later…"

"Maybe," she said. "Oh, Leo, I appreciate your understanding more than I can say! I don't want you to think I take your friendship lightly. It's just…can we keep it there for now?"

"Of course. I don't want to make you uncomfortable."

Despite his assurances, Diane could tell he felt hurt by her refusal. When they had hung up, she sat still for a moment and pulled in a deep breath. Tears filled her eyes. She dashed them away, angry with herself.

Time to admit she was going through a blue period. Of course her illness and medication affected her emotions, but she felt it was more than that. Valentine's Day was such a trigger. It brought back memories of precious times with Eric. Maybe his death was still influencing her when it came to relationships, though she had thought she was past that. One thing she'd learned was that grief could assail you suddenly and powerfully, in many guises. She leaned back and closed her eyes. Maybe this was a topic to explore on her blog—when she felt better, of course. The thought that Leo might read it and be even more hurt, even if she didn't mention his name, made her think better of that idea.

Right now all she knew for certain was that the holiday carried too much baggage for her. She needed—or wanted anyway—to be alone on Valentine's Day and not feel pressured by anyone else's expectations. She didn't like to think she might be stifling a potentially wonderful friendship because she didn't feel good. Maybe when the holiday was over, she could calmly consider spending more time with Leo.

"Lord, I know You'll bring me through this," she whispered. "It's one of those things that keeps coming back. Please give me strength emotionally, as well as physically."

A moist nose nuzzled her hand, and she opened her eyes. Rocky was nudging her.

She couldn't help but smile. "Hello, boy. Thanks for caring." She stroked his head and neck, thankful for this quiet companion who faithfully stuck by her, asking little in return.

* * *

Margaret had come to a decision by Friday morning. Her Valentine's surprise for Allan would be a special meal, which she would prepare herself. The plan was ambitious, considering that she wasn't much of a cook. But everyone seemed to have plans involving a romantic dinner. She knew that if she put her mind to it, she could make their holiday evening one to remember. Allan would be so proud of her.

During a lull at the gallery, she began to search online for the perfect dishes to fill out her menu. Asparagus-and-mozzarella-stuffed chicken breasts sounded good, but she wasn't sure she could get fresh asparagus at this time of year. She bookmarked the recipe and kept looking, until the bell over the front door jingled.

She breezed out of her office. Diane had just come in, sans dog this time.

"Hello," Margaret said. "How lovely to see you again."

"Hey." Diane smiled. "It's been so nice out this week, I've been taking advantage of it. I'm meeting Augie at the Cove, but I was fifteen minutes early, so I thought I'd pop in and see how you were doing."

"It's been slow this week," Margaret said, but as the words left her mouth, the door opened again and two women came in.

Diane stepped discreetly to the side and studied a seascape painting on the wall. Margaret moved forward to greet the newcomers.

"Good morning! Mrs. Bernard, isn't it?"

"Yes," the silver-haired woman said. "My sister-in-law has been raving about the painting I bought here last fall, so I brought her in. Do you have anything by the same artist?"

"I believe we do," Margaret said. "That was a Dorothy Granger, wasn't it?"

"Oh my, you have a good memory!" Mrs. Bernard waved her hand. "Yes, it's a lovely view of an old hay rake in a thicket of raspberry bushes. It reminded me of my father's old farm."

"I assure you my memory's like a sieve most days," Margaret said with a chuckle, "but Dorothy is a friend, and she's one of my favorite artists." She glanced toward Diane, who was heading quietly toward the door. "Goodbye, Diane," she called.

Diane waved and smiled, then slipped outside. A half hour later, Mrs. Bernard's friend walked out with a Dorothy Granger landscape, this one featuring a rustic barn and a glimpse of distant tide flats. Margaret was pleased with the sale, and Dorothy would be delighted too, but she hadn't forgotten that she only had six days to plan and produce the most elaborate meal of her life. When she was sure the ladies had driven off, she scurried back to her office and once more sat down at her computer.

★ ★ ★

Augie Jackson was just entering the Cove when Diane got there, with a furry Cossack hat covering his bald head. He saw her and paused outside the door.

"Well, good day to you!" His big white mustache twitched as he pushed open the door and held it for her.

"Thanks, Augie. How are you?"

"Doing fine," he said.

They went in and stood in front of the counter. Brenna was serving a young man, and Diane recognized one of Shelley's raspberry scones as part of his order.

She leaned toward Augie. "Why do I have this sudden craving for scones?"

He laughed. "Every time I come into this place, I get a craving for something sweet."

They ordered their hot drinks and pastries and then found a small table near the window. Augie took off his jacket and fur hat, placing them on an empty chair. Diane unzipped her parka, but kept it on. She took off her knit gloves and stuffed them in her pockets.

"Oh, your Danish looks good! Maybe I should have gotten one of those."

Augie's eyes twinkled. "I'll split it with you, if you give me part of your scone."

They settled the transaction, and Diane bit into her half of the scone first. "*Mmm,* that's good."

Augie leaned over and pulled a small book out of the pocket of his jacket. "Are you ready for some good reading, as well as good food?"

Diane felt the excitement that came when she researched for a book and stumbled across a nugget of information beyond what she'd dreamed of—or when she unearthed another clue to a real-life mystery.

"What did you find?"

Augie held out the volume. "This is about industry in Maine. The chapter on the limestone trade mentions the quarry here in Marble Cove."

Diane took the book and opened it to the table of contents. "Just a mention, or something pithier?"

"Well, the author did allude to there being a scandal attached to our quarry, and I vaguely remember when that happened. He didn't go into detail, though. Read it and see what you think. But you had said something to me about Elias Thorpe, and I thought you'd find it interesting—they mention him as an investor in the quarry."

"You thought right. I'm interested in anything to do with Elias Thorpe. Thanks, Augie!"

"Always a pleasure. Now tell me how your new book is going."

Diane settled back and took a sip of her mocha coffee. As much as she would like to hurry home and dive into this book, she knew Augie loved to talk, and to listen to others tell what they were up to. Recounting her recent wrestling with the plot of her new book would be a small way to repay him for all his kindnesses. More than once, Augie had pointed her to a valuable piece of information concerning the town's past.

An hour later, she walked slowly home. The temperature was cooling, and her legs were tired. The morning out had drained her reserves of energy. She'd eat lunch and then lie down for a while with Augie's book. Of course, Rocky would be peeved that she hadn't taken him with her this morning. She'd have to take him out for a run this afternoon, but right now that idea just made her fatigue more noticeable.

When she arrived at the cottage, she let Rocky out into the yard for a few minutes. By the time she could coax him inside again, she was ready to collapse. Knowing her blood sugar was not to be trifled with, she drank a small glass of juice and then tumbled onto her bed with the green cloth-bound book in hand. Maybe she would just close her eyes for a few minutes before she started reading. She pulled the extra blanket over her.

She awoke suddenly and lifted her head. The clock said two-fifteen. She had slept for more than three hours. Rocky gave a little whine, and she realized it was probably this that had awakened her. He stood at the edge of the bed, his nose lying on the coverlet and his big brown eyes regarding her mournfully.

"Okay, boy. I hear you." She sat up and stretched. So much for all that reading she was going to do. By this time, she was quite hungry. She shoved her feet into her slippers and rose. "Come on, Rocky. Let's see what we've got to eat."

In the kitchen, she opened a can of soup and put it into a bowl she could heat in the microwave. While she waited for it to warm, she fixed herself a glass of water and a small salad. Then she gave Rocky a treat.

"We'll walk, boy, I promise. Let me get something into my stomach first."

As soon as she ate some of the hearty soup, she felt better. However, the air had continued to cool outside, and she bundled up with a woolly scarf and a knit hat she could pull down over her ears. Instead of the long romp on the beach she'd planned, she and Rocky stayed out only about twenty minutes. The cutting wind off the bay now made strolling uncomfortable. She hoped they weren't in for a big storm.

Rocky seemed to revel in the outing—when they reached the end of the boardwalk to the beach, he tore around her in wide circles. But Diane felt too shaky to move fast enough to keep warm. She was glad when Rocky was willing to end the walk early.

Once back at the house, she at last settled in to read the chapter on quarrying in Augie's book. Intrigued by the author's brief touch on the scandal surrounding the business at the quarry, she wished for more. The information was just enough to make Diane suspicious of Elias Thorpe's involvement in the company that mined the limestone. It seemed the scandal involved money. While the author didn't spell things out, she had the impression that the company's management had done some creative accounting.

She took some notes, planning to share the information with her friends, especially Margaret, who was a retired accountant. Perhaps she would have an idea as to what the scandal involved.

The little book was a welcome distraction from her health and career concerns, and Diane browsed two or three more chapters, fascinated by the variety of industry in Maine in the last two centuries.

Finally she went to her computer. She wasn't in the mental gear to work on her mystery novel, but she could write a new blog post this afternoon. She mentioned in her short essay that she was a bit down, and some days felt discouraged at the slowness of her recovery, even though she believed God had taken her cancer away. One of the biggest blessings she'd experienced throughout her illness was the loving support of friends and family. Today Margaret and Augie, and even Rocky, had shored her up. She ended the post with praise to God for His goodness—no matter how low she felt, God never changed, and He always upheld her.

* * *

Shelley waited until she and Dan had tucked Emma and Aiden into bed and Hailey was settled down to write a letter to her mother before bringing up the subject of the Cove.

"Boy, I don't know," Dan said, frowning. "Does he want you to buy the place *now*? I thought that was something to think about way down the road."

"He knows we don't have that kind of money. I'm not sure what he has in mind, since he revised his timetable for retirement. Maybe he'd keep the ownership and just hire me as the manager for a couple of years."

Dan sighed. "I'm sure you could do it, Shell, but wouldn't you be spreading yourself kind of thin?"

"That's what I'm worried about." She sighed and leaned back on the couch, hugging a squishy blue throw pillow against her chest. "I really would like to help Rusty out, and I'd love to own my own store, but I'm not sure this is the right thing for our family. When we talked about it a few months ago, we decided that it could be a possibility in the future, but not this soon."

"Exactly," Dan said. "I mean, we've got Hailey to think about, and who would take care of Emma while you were at the Cove?"

"That would be something to consider. I don't know if the extra money would cover child care expenses and still be worthwhile."

"Do you *want* to be over there every day? I know you always wanted your own bakery, but still—"

"This could be the perfect situation," she said. "It's already a thriving business. I could keep the coffee shop and expand the bakery part."

"I don't know, Shell…The timing seems off to me."

Shelley leaned over and kissed the worry lines creasing Dan's forehead. "Let's not decide tonight, okay? Right now I'm leaning toward thinking it would take me away from the kids too much."

They sat looking at each other for a long moment.

"Let's pray about it," Shelley suggested.

"Okay. And whatever you decide, I'll try to help you make it work."

She couldn't ask for more than that. Shelley snuggled into his arms. "Do you need to study?"

"Yeah, I need to take the next test in my electronics course this week."

"Right. I'll be in the kitchen working on the Valentine cookie orders. If Hailey comes out here, tell her I could use her help putting the boxes together, would you?"

"Sure." Dan kissed her and let her go.

Shelley smiled as she rose from the couch. "Thanks. And let's think about Rusty's offer for a couple days at least."

CHAPTER FOUR

Margaret made it through the fox-trot with Allan on the third song without tripping. When the music stopped, they clapped with the other students. Margaret was inordinately proud of them. They had come a long way in their proficiency.

The instructor paused the CD player and faced them.

"That was pretty good! Let's do one more fox-trot, and then I'll let you go back to the waltz for our last number tonight. I'm really pleased with what you're all doing. Although, Steve, you need to watch your footwork." She smiled at Steve's wife. "Lou, if you'll let me borrow your husband for a minute, I'll work on that with him. But I promise I'll give him right back."

Everyone laughed. As the strains of Frank Sinatra's "Fly Me to the Moon" filled the air, Allan turned to Margaret and held out his hands. "Shall we?"

Their dance went fairly well, and the instructor came by, eyeing them critically, about halfway through the number.

"Good, Margaret," she said. "Think tall. Shoulders up, chin high."

Margaret always thought "thinking tall" was a bit of a strain for shorties like her, but she straightened and managed to get an extra half inch or so out of her lazy spine. Allan hummed along with Sinatra in his own mellow tones, gazing into her eyes.

"I think this was a good idea," she said softly.

"You got that right."

When the song was over, the instructor went to the front and applauded them. "You all are doing great! Don't forget, Valentine's Day is Thursday. That's only six days away, folks. I think all of you are ready to take your dancing out in public, at least for the waltz and fox-trot. If anyone's not sure and you want a private brushup session, speak to me after our last number."

She put on the dreamy waltz, and Allan took Margaret into his arms again.

"Do you want to go out dancing Thursday?" he asked.

"Me? I don't think so. I'm not as confident as our teacher seems to be. Besides, I had something else in mind." She looked up at him from beneath her lashes. If only her special gourmet meal came off as well as these lessons! Maybe they'd dance afterward, in their own living room.

"Oh? Like what?" Allan asked.

"It's a surprise, but save the evening for me, okay?"

"Are you asking me to be your valentine?"

"Absolutely."

"Then the answer is yes." Allan stooped and brushed his lips across her hair.

So far so good, Margaret thought, resisting the urge to cross her fingers.

★ ★ ★

On Saturday morning, the four friends gathered in Diane's sunny kitchen for coffee. The aqua walls with oyster-white trim kept the cottage feeling like a summer haven all year long. Shelley had brought butterscotch chip cookies, and they all fixed their beverages and gathered around the table.

Beverly said, "I meant to get more research done on the Thorpe house this week, but I got caught up in some work for a client, and I really didn't get much done. Diane, what's your news?"

Diane smiled and touched the small green book that lay in the middle of the table. "I've been reading about the quarry out by the depot. It was quite a going concern in the 1940s and 1950s."

"I asked Frances about it," Shelley said. "She thought Elias Thorpe had worked at the quarry for a while, or that he was involved in the management—or something to do with it anyway. She wasn't really sure what."

"Augie's book should be a help," Diane said. "It has a list of six original investors in the business. They put up capital to pay for the equipment that was needed."

"Did they own the property that the quarry was on?" Beverly asked.

"No—remember the Gentry brothers? They owned it up until it closed, but these other men invested in the business. When the opportunity to sell a lot of stone came up, I'm thinking they were short on cash and approached these others to help finance the operation. The Gentrys moved away after the quarry shut down."

"I'll see what else I can find out," Beverly said. "I did learn that the Inglewoods have a hired caretaker who looks after the Thorpe house when they go to Florida each winter. His name is Willard Rockwell, and I have his phone number, but I haven't contacted him. It's not much, but I thought he might know something about the house's history."

"Sounds like a possibility," Margaret said. "Do you plan to call him?"

"I think I will. In fact, I could make the call today, while we're all here, if you think it's a good idea." Beverly looked around at the others.

"Sure," Shelley said. "Go for it."

"Use my landline if you want," Diane offered.

Beverly walked to the counter and took down the wall phone. She put in the number and waited. Diane went over and placed a notepad and pen conveniently nearby.

But a moment later, Beverly turned to face them, frowning. "No answer."

"Oh well, you tried," Diane said. She picked up the coffeepot and made the rounds, topping off everyone's cup.

"So, what's everyone doing Thursday, for Valentine's Day?" Shelley asked.

"Jeff's taking me out to dinner," Beverly said. As usual, she stayed calm and poised, but Diane noted a gleam in her eyes when she mentioned her fiancé.

"Super," Shelley said. "We're going out too."

"Well, Allan and I are staying in," Margaret said. "Don't breathe a word, but I'm fixing a surprise for him."

"What is it?" Diane asked.

"A fancy gourmet dinner. I've been hunting up recipes and making a shopping list a mile long."

"Fun," Shelley said.

Diane wondered about that. Cooking was not Margaret's strong suit. In fact, she had frequently stated that she hated cooking, and Allan had done most of it in all the years of their marriage. If nothing else, it would certainly be a surprise to him.

"How about you, Diane?" Beverly asked. "Do you have plans?"

"No, I..." Margaret threw her a sympathetic look, and Diane decided she could come clean with her friends. Doing that might even help her to feel better about it. "Leo asked me out, but I just didn't feel good about it, so I told him no."

"You need to do what you think is best," Margaret said softly.

"Thanks."

"But you like him, right?" Shelley pressed.

"Well, sure. He's a good friend. But I don't think I want it to go further than that right now. At least not until I feel completely better and I'm back to myself. Whatever that is." She laughed.

"Is it your illness?" Beverly asked. "You've been doing so well."

"It may be partly that." Diane felt the urge to squirm as the three watched her.

"You and Leo get along so well. I thought over Christmas that I saw a few sparks. So, what are you afraid of?" Shelley asked soberly.

Diane looked down into her mug. "I don't know. Some of it may be just the idea of being part of a couple again. I admit, I have moments when I think of Leo in a romantic way, but somehow I don't feel as if I should let those feelings grow right now."

"Then wait until you're sure," Margaret said. "That's my philosophy. When in doubt, wait."

Beverly nodded. "It's better not to get into something than to jump in and have to get yourself out of it later."

Shelley sighed. "I guess I'm just a romantic at heart. I want everyone to be happy."

"I'm happy," Diane said. "I have a lot to be happy about." She smiled at Shelley. "You three are some of my biggest blessings."

Margaret reached over and squeezed her hand. "We're all here for you."

"Yes," Beverly said. "And don't hesitate to ask for help if you need it."

"Now that you mention it…I wasn't going to ask, because I know you're all busy, but it would be nice to have someone go with me to my treatment Monday."

"I'd love to take you," Beverly said at once. "Is it at the same time you've been going?"

"Yes. They changed the day, but it's at the same time and I'll only have two this month."

Beverly nodded.

"Thanks so much," Diane said.

Shelley came over and gave Diane a hug. "These guys are right. About Leo, I mean. And whatever you decide, I support you. Don't make any big decisions while you're low."

"That's right," Margaret said. "This is a time to nurture yourself. Pamper yourself, even. I know that's hard for you to do sometimes, but you need to take care of yourself."

"Let us take care of you too," Shelley said. "I'll pop over Monday to see how you're doing."

"Thank you." These wonderful friends had become part of Diane's family, and she basked in their supportive friendship as they moved on to other topics. God had truly blessed her when she moved to Newport Avenue.

★ ★ ★

That evening, Shelley was startled to receive a phone call from Rusty Garrison. Dan and the children had settled cozily in the living room to watch a video together, and Shelley was in the kitchen when the phone rang, going over her list of cookie customers. She would start shipping the Valentine gift boxes on Monday and wanted to be sure she hadn't missed anything.

"Shelley?" Rusty asked. "How's it going?"

"Fine," she said, trying to gauge his voice and discern the reason for his unprecedented call. "Is everything okay at the Cove?"

"Fine and dandy. I just wondered if you've spoken to Dan yet."

"Well, yeah, some," Shelley said. Her stomach started roiling. That couldn't be a good sign.

"Listen," Rusty said. "Wendy and I have decided to take a vacation. I'm really frazzled, and we both need to get where it's warm and sunny for a while, you know?"

"Uh…that sounds like fun, Rusty. When are you going?"

"In a week and a half. The eighteenth. We've booked a cruise."

"A cruise?" It sounded better and better, but she wasn't sure what Rusty and Wendy's cruise had to do with her.

"Yeah. In the Caribbean. Lots of sun. And I wondered if you could run the store while I'm gone."

Ah, there it was. She sat down on a stool at the island and hauled in a deep breath. "Uh…well…tell me more. What would I have to do?"

"Oh, just everything." Rusty laughed. "It wouldn't be that hard. Brenna could even open up some mornings if you needed her to. You'd have to stay until closing every night, though."

"Hmm. I don't know. How long is this for?"

"Just six days."

Shelley looked up as Dan entered the kitchen. He looked at her questioningly.

"Rusty, can I call you back?" Shelley asked. "I need to talk to Dan about this."

"I need to know tonight."

"Okay, I'll get back to you. Dan's right here. Just give us ten minutes or so."

"Okay," Rusty said and hung up.

"What's up?" Dan asked as he filled a glass with milk. "Is he pressuring you about the deal he offered?"

"No, he's pressuring me about a different deal. Rusty and his wife are going on a cruise starting the eighteenth. They'll be gone about a week. He wants me to run the Cove while he's away."

Dan paused with the milk jug in his hands. "Might not be a bad idea."

"Really?" Shelley asked.

"It would be kind of a trial run. Might be a good way to see what it would be like to own the business."

Shelley could hardly believe he was encouraging her to do it. "I suppose so," she said slowly. "And I'd be done with the Valentine cookies by then."

"Sure. If it went okay and you really liked doing it full-time, we could seriously think about the other offer. But if you hate it, then you'll know, and you can tell him to start looking for someone else to take over when he retires. No hard feelings."

"Yeah, maybe so." Shelley glanced at the calendar. "Do you know yet where you'll be working that week?"

"Not for sure. I'll ask Wayne. Things have been a little slow, so maybe I can get some time off that week."

"That would be great, because I can't take Emma with me, and Hailey's too young to leave alone with the kids."

Dan put the milk back in the refrigerator and shut the door. "Well, my mom would keep Emma if you needed her to."

"I'm sure she would," Shelley said. They looked at each other for a moment.

"Right," Dan said. "It's only a week."

"Well, if I took it on full-time, we'd need other arrangements. For sure."

"Agreed."

She sat motionless while Dan helped himself to a poppy seed muffin from her "rejects" container.

"So…should I call Rusty back and tell him I'll do it while he's off on the cruise?"

"Only if you want to."

"I think I do. I mean, I always dreamed of having my own business—a storefront bakery—but I didn't have the confidence to try it."

"Or the cash," Dan put in.

"Yeah. I might love it."

"You might."

She nodded. "I'll do it."

Dan came over and kissed her. "Let me know if you need me to talk to Mom." He took his muffin and glass of milk and headed for the living room.

It probably wouldn't be long before the children came to the kitchen wanting a snack. Shelley picked up the phone and returned Rusty's call.

"Hey, Shelley," he said when he picked it up.

"Hey. It's okay. I'll do it for that one week. It will be a good opportunity to find out if I want to go ahead with the business."

"Great. When you bring the pastries some morning this week, I'll go over everything with you."

"Sounds good." A moment later, Shelley hung up with a strange mixture of anticipation and dread filling her. What had she gotten herself into?

* * *

Diane had to force herself to get dressed Sunday morning and go out for the church service. Maybe she had overdone yesterday—her fatigue seemed worse than it had been for several days. She had gone down to the beach with Shelley and the kids, along with Rocky and Prize. The children and the dogs had loved the outing. Diane had grown tired long before they headed home, but she hadn't wanted to say anything. Now she could see how foolish that was. Shelley would have understood if she had cut the walk short.

She sat with one of the other members of the Lay Ministries Committee. Diane hadn't been able to take part much in that outreach, but she kept up with the committee's doings.

Pastor Carl's sermon spoke to her heart, and she was glad she had made the effort to attend. After she got home and rested a while, she decided to work on her blog. Several supportive comments had come in since she had last checked it, and her heart warmed. She truly had been blessed with friends, both those on her street and the ones she only knew online.

Tomorrow was the day for her next scheduled treatment. She hoped she didn't start out the day feeling poorly. Knowing Beverly would be at her side encouraged her.

Inspiration for a blog entry came to her: she could post about how wonderful her friends had been, without naming names, and tell how their help and prayers had sustained her. She picked up her Bible to hunt for a Scripture or two to go with her thoughts.

As she turned the pages of Isaiah, she found a highlighted passage she loved in the forty-third chapter: *When thou passest through the waters, I will be with thee; and through the rivers, they shall not overflow thee: when thou walkest through the fire, thou shalt not be burned; neither shall the flame kindle upon thee. For I am the LORD thy God, the Holy One of Israel, thy Saviour.*

Though the words were written to the Israelites thousands of years ago, Diane didn't hesitate to claim them for her own. She had passed through the waters and walked through the fire. Even though her body had suffered, she knew God was still protecting her, and He would always be with her.

"Because of that," she wrote, "I'm not afraid to die. I'm glad I've beaten the cancer again, but even if I hadn't, I know this life is not the end."

She sat back in her chair, exhausted yet comforted.

CHAPTER FIVE

Beverly went up to Diane's door and knocked softly. She didn't want to push herself on Diane, but if her friend needed a little extra help this morning, she wanted to be on the spot. Diane opened the door with a wan smile.

"Hi. I'm ready to go. I just need to get my coat."

Beverly stepped inside to wait. Diane moved slowly as she rigged up for the cold weather.

"It's only fifteen degrees this morning," Beverly said. "You'll probably want a hat too."

"The whole ensemble, eh?" Diane chuckled and knotted an ombré scarf loosely around her neck. "Leo called last night."

"Oh?" Beverly eyed her carefully. "Everything all right?"

"Yes. He remembered that this was my treatment day, and he offered to take me. It was sweet of him, but I told him you've been taking me and we'd already arranged it. I'm not sure I could hold up if he was there with me all morning."

Beverly had a strong impulse to hug Diane. At first she held back, thinking that would be too intrusive, too emotional. But as Diane fitted a knit cap over her glossy brown hair, Beverly caught the shimmer of tears in her eyes. Pushing down her long-nourished inhibitions, she took a step forward and held out her arms.

Diane stepped into her embrace with a rueful chuckle. "Dear Beverly! Thank you so much! I needed someone like you this morning. No, I take that back. I needed *you*. And God knew that."

Beverly gave her a gentle squeeze and stepped back. "I'm glad I could come."

"You'll probably be bored with waiting."

"I brought my e-reader, as usual. Are you ready?"

Diane nodded.

"Come on then." Beverly walked with her out to the car and drove the familiar route to the cancer center in Augusta. The roads were bare, thanks to plowing and sanding the town had done after the last snow, and the days of warmth that had melted the last of the ice on the pavement.

In the waiting room, they chatted about the services at their churches the previous day, and about the mystery surrounding the old train station and the eerie train whistles the four friends heard now and then.

To Beverly's surprise, when Diane was called into the treatment room, she was allowed to go with her. The nurse made sure an extra chair was placed nearby for Beverly. Diane sat down in a padded recliner chair to receive her medication. The experimental treatment seemed to be working for her, and Beverly was glad Diane's doctor had suggested it.

Half a dozen other patients had also come in for their treatments and sat in recliners about the perimeter of the room. The nurses moved about, adjusting IV drips and bringing pillows and other comfort items.

"Are you comfortable?" the cheerful, dark-haired nurse whose nametag read Cheryl asked Diane when her treatment had begun.

Diane nodded with a smile, but to Beverly she looked drawn. She hated to see her friend go into the treatment already fatigued. According to Diane's doctor, the cancer was now at bay, but the long ordeal had taken its toll, and Diane would need time, rest, and good nutrition to bring her back to full health.

The nurse asked her a few more questions, focusing mostly on her diet and hypoglycemia, and then she brought a meter and tested Diane's blood sugar.

"Looks like you're doing okay," she said, smiling. "Can I get you anything now? You can have some juice if you'd like. Or some herbal tea, maybe?"

"No, thanks," Diane said. "Maybe later."

Cheryl nodded and looked at Beverly. "How about you? May I bring you something?"

"No, thank you," Beverly said. "I'll just sit with Diane if that's okay."

"That's perfect. Let me know if either of you needs anything."

Beverly kept up a quiet conversation for a few minutes, but when Diane leaned her head back and closed her eyes, she kept quiet. After a couple of minutes, she took her e-reader from her purse and opened it to a document she needed to read to help her make informed decisions about a client's account. Diane dozed for half an hour and only awoke when the nurse came to check her progress.

"Oh goodness, did I sleep?" she asked, blinking at Beverly.

"Yes, and I think that's a good thing. Don't be embarrassed."

"Okay, I won't." Diane shifted in her chair. "I always feel so helpless on treatment days. It's so…not *me*."

Beverly smiled. "I know. But it gives the rest of us a chance to spoil you."

When they left the hospital, Diane walked as steadily as she had when they arrived. Beverly made sure she was securely buckled into the passenger seat and took her place behind the wheel.

"Is there any place you'd like to stop on the way home?" she asked.

Diane shook her head. "I think a good nap is in order."

"Okay, but don't forget to eat lunch. You didn't have anything at the hospital, so you probably need to eat something soon."

"You're right. Thanks."

At Diane's house, Beverly insisted she eat, and Diane decided after a moment's indecision that she could eat half a turkey sandwich.

Beverly placed the sandwich plate on the table. "How about some juice with that?"

"I guess so."

Beverly found a bottle of cran-raspberry juice in the refrigerator and poured a small glass. She took it to the table and sat down opposite Diane.

"Here you go."

"Thanks," Diane said. "Do you think we can really save the train station? We keep talking about it, but we don't seem to be making much progress."

"I know," Beverly said. "I'd hate to see us lose another little piece of Marble Cove history—even though Dennis' project would bring jobs to Marble Cove."

Diane shrugged as she took a bite of her sandwich. A moment later, she said, "What can we do, besides waiting for the Inglewoods to come back from Florida? I'm not convinced that we'll find any worthwhile clues in Elias Thorpe's old house. He hasn't lived there for what—sixty years? Surely the owners between then and now would have found anything significant."

"You never know," Beverly said. "But there are a few other things we can do. For instance, I want to do more research on the station itself. If we want to block Dennis from destroying it, we need to convince people that it's a meaningful part of this town's heritage. I'll keep digging at the town office."

"Maybe there are more articles in the newspaper archives too," Diane said. "We had to cut our search short in the fall."

"Good point. We could look back and see if there are notices of any famous people arriving in town by train, for instance."

"Yeah! It would be neat to find an old picture of a famous person at the train station. That's a great idea. I wish I could do more to help with this."

"You just focus on getting better," Beverly said. "I'm really proud of the way you've fought this thing. But you need to rest."

"I know you're right. I want to be up and doing things, but my body just won't cooperate."

Twenty minutes later, Beverly tucked Diane into bed. Her face was pale against the snowy pillowcase.

"I'm going to take Rocky out for a few minutes, and then I'll leave, but I'll call you later," Beverly said. "And when you get some strength back, maybe we can dive into this whole thing about the quarry too."

"Oh, I almost forgot." Diane sat up. "Take my notebook. It's the one right beside the keyboard on my desk. I made some notes in it about the quarry. Stuff from Augie's book, and a little bit I found online, but that wasn't much."

"I'll get it," Beverly said. "After lunch, I'm going over to the municipal building, and if I have a chance, I'll ask Angela to pull some records on the quarry for me."

"Great," Diane murmured, sinking back on her pillow. Her eyelids were already drooping.

Beverly took Rocky out for a ten-minute romp in the yard. She would be late getting home for lunch. Mrs. Peabody wouldn't be happy about that, but she would understand. Shelley's white Outback wagon rolled down the street and turned in at their driveway, the last one on the left.

Shelley got out of the car and removed Emma from her car seat in the rear seat. As she straightened with the toddler in her arms, Shelley spotted Beverly and waved.

"Hey, Beverly! Was Diane's treatment this morning?" Shelley called.

Beverly nodded.

Shelley walked toward her, so Beverly fastened Diane's gate with Rocky enclosed in the yard and walked across to the end of the Bauers' driveway.

"I told her I'd take Rocky out for a few minutes if she'd lie down," she told Shelley. "I don't suppose you could check on her later—say three o'clock or so?"

"Of course," Shelley said. "We just got home from a trip to the market. I'll run over and see Diane when Hailey gets home from school. Is Diane okay?"

"I think she's just tired out. But I'll feel better if someone looks in on her in a few hours. And I'll give her a call this evening. I don't want to smother her, but..."

"I know what you mean," Shelley said. "It's a little scary."

* * *

Diane was up and sitting at her computer when the doorbell rang late that afternoon. Rocky had been dozing on the rug in her office, but he sat up and barked at the chime.

"Take it easy," Diane said. She rose and walked out to open the door. Shelley stood on the small front porch with two travel mugs in her hands.

"Hope I didn't wake you up."

"No, I was looking over the last chapter I did on my book and trying to get motivated to write some more. Hard to believe I'm actually writing my third book."

Shelley grinned and held out one of the mugs. "I know—it's fantastic. How about a hot cocoa break? Adelaide's with the kids for a little while. I've got butterscotch cookie bars in a bag in my pocket."

Diane laughed. "You are determined to fatten me up, aren't you? I'd love to take a break with you. Come right in."

She led Shelley to the living room, where they set their mugs on coasters on the coffee table. Before removing her puffy down parka, Shelley extracted a plastic zipper bag of cookie bars from one side pocket and set it between the mugs. Then she peeled off the parka and laid it on one of the chairs.

"Hey, it's cold out!"

Diane burst out in laughter. "Shelley, you're good medicine."

"Thanks."

"How's your business doing?"

"Good," Shelley said. "Almost too good."

"Oh?" Diane cautiously sipped the hot chocolate through the slit in the travel mug's top. "That's delicious."

"Thanks. Gourmet white chocolate blend—I'm trying it out for Rusty. I'll tell him you approve. So, business." Shelley sat down and slapped the knees of her jeans. "I'm doing Valentine cookies, you know."

"Yes, you mentioned that."

"Well, it's a bumper crop this year. I got half again as many orders as last year."

"Wow," Diane said. "Is that a problem?"

"Not really. Hailey's been helping me put the boxes together. I shipped the first ones this morning—the ones that need to go the farthest. And another big batch will go out tomorrow. Local ones I'll save for Wednesday." Shelley sipped her cocoa.

"It sounds like you have things under control," Diane said.

"Yeah, with that. But did I tell you about what Rusty wants me to do?"

"No. What?"

Shelley sighed. "He wants to retire this spring. As in before Memorial Day, when the summer rush starts."

"I didn't know that," Diane said. "Wow. That's soon."

"Yeah, and he has what he thinks is a brilliant plan to keep the Cove going."

"I'm guessing it involves you?"

Shelley nodded. "In a big way. He wants me to take it over."

"You mean…buy the business? I thought that was off in the distant future."

"It was, but now he wants to retire earlier. He knows Dan and I couldn't afford to buy it now, but he thinks we could work something out. He and his wife want to travel a lot, and he's tired of being in the store all day."

"That makes sense," Diane said, thinking of how she and Eric had been cheated out of the retirement time they'd dreamed of together. "He probably should do it now, while he's able to enjoy it."

"That's what he said. But I'm not sure it's the right direction for me."

Diane nodded slowly. "I can see why."

"Can you?" Shelley asked eagerly. "I sort of felt like I should do it, like I owe Rusty something. He's been so supportive, and he's been my main customer since the very beginning. He let me use his kitchen all those months..."

"Rusty is a very nice man," Diane said carefully, "but that doesn't mean you're obligated to carry out his dream for him."

"Well, it's sort of my dream too. I always wanted a bakery, but I didn't really think about its being in a coffee shop."

"You've had a good business relationship with Rusty, and it worked for both of you," Diane said. "But this is different."

"Very different." Shelley sipped her cocoa. "I'm going to give it a sort of audition. But I haven't promised him anything."

"That sounds like a good idea. Tell me about it." Diane picked up the plastic bag and took out a cookie bar.

"Rusty and Wendy are leaving the eighteenth on a cruise," Shelley said. "That week, I'm going to manage the Cove. Brenna will help me, and Rusty's got a couple of other part-timers too. We'll see how it goes. If I think it will work out, maybe I'll go ahead with it this spring. But there are a lot of things to consider, the kids being the biggest."

"Absolutely. Have you worked that out for the trial period?"

"Not completely. Dan's going to try to get some shorter hours that week. But if I did this all summer, he couldn't take time off to help with the kids. So that really is the one major roadblock. That and…" Shelley let the thought trail off and shook her head, sending her blonde hair rippling.

"That and what?"

Shelley looked soberly into her eyes. "I don't know if I could run the Cove and my bakery business, and still have time with my family. Dan says that one-week trial will help us decide."

"Lots to think about. I'll be praying for you and Dan." Diane took a bite of the cookie bar, and sweet butterscotch bathed her mouth. "Mmm, that's good. If I try to eat another one, slap my hand, though."

"You can keep the rest for later," Shelley said. "So how's it going with Leo? I'm sorry if I made you feel uncomfortable about that topic."

"We're okay. I think he feels a little hurt, and I admit I feel guilty. But that's better than raising his expectations, right?"

"Right! You don't have any reason to feel bad, Diane. If you don't want to see the guy, you should just tell him, and that will be that."

Diane considered her words while she sipped her cocoa. "The truth is, I don't want to shut him out completely. I like Leo. But I don't want there to be any awkwardness over the status of our relationship. Maybe that's not possible at this stage."

Diane's house phone rang.

"I'm sorry," she said. "Let me check the caller ID." She rose and went to her desk. "It's Jessica."

"I'm outta here," Shelley said, scooping up the travel mugs. "Great talking to you, Diane!"

Diane smiled and waved at her as she picked up the phone. "Hello, honey. How's it going?"

Rocky followed Shelley out of the room, but Diane knew her friend would shut him in securely—Shelley was used to dogs. She turned her full attention to her daughter.

"Hi, Mom! I was wondering what you'd decided about Valentine's Day. Are you going out with Leo?"

"I—no. No, I decided not to."

"*Mo-om!*"

Diane had to smile. "It's better this way. Trust me."

Jessica sighed, and Diane felt it was necessary to hash through her dilemma again with her daughter. She wanted Jessica to understand, but she also wanted to remain firm.

"Okay," Jessica said at last. "Just keep in mind that one date a year doesn't obligate you to have a romantic relationship with the guy. You can be friends and go on supporting each other without being in love."

"I know you're right, honey. And I'm not ready to say that I'll never fall in love with Leo. But I'm also not ready to lock into an exclusive relationship with him."

"Sounds like you might be having a few regrets," Jessica said. "Do you wish you'd said yes?"

"Not really. I had my treatment this morning, and that always leaves me a little depleted. The timing just isn't right for me now."

"I'm sorry," Jessica said quickly. "I should have asked you first how you felt physically."

"That's okay." Diane sank down on the sofa cradling the phone. "I'm doing fine. But I still think I was right not to commit to going out on Thursday. When I feel better I'll think this over thoroughly."

"Sure," Jessica said. "And it's not like you can't call him sometime and ask him to do something with you."

"Right. So...how's Martin?"

"Not good."

Diane straightened. "Oh, Jessica, I'm sorry. What's happened?"

"Nothing, really, but I'm worried, Mom."

"What is it? There must be something specific that's got you on edge."

"Well, yeah. He just...Every time I try to talk to him about setting the date, or who we want in the wedding party—anything wedding-related—he changes the subject. I'm starting to wonder if he's having second thoughts about marrying me, Mom." Jessica's voice broke, sending a pang through Diane's heart.

"Oh, sweetie, that's probably not true. I'm sure he has reasons. Maybe he's just preoccupied with stuff from work."

"I don't think that's it."

"Okay," Diane said, trying to keep her voice even. "Maybe you should just bring it up head-on. Tell him how it worries you."

"Maybe. I don't want to nag him, but he won't open up to me. If I try to talk about it, he's off on another tack. I had sort of decided not to bring up anything about the wedding until *he* does."

"I wish I could help," Diane said. Jessica sounded so forlorn that she was tempted to jump in her car and drive to Boston, but she knew she wasn't up to that. "I'll certainly keep praying about this," she said.

"That's all you can do."

CHAPTER SIX

Shelley took her pastries to the Cove early on Tuesday morning, before Dan had to leave for work and Hailey for school. Rusty was just opening the back entrance when she arrived.

"Hey," he called. "Glad you made it. Let me start the coffee and we can go over some things."

Shelley removed the stale pastries from the display cases and restocked them with fresh ones while Rusty did his early morning "must do" routine.

"Okay," he said a few minutes later. "Come on out back. We've got fifteen minutes before I open for business."

In the familiar kitchen, Shelley felt right at home. She wouldn't have any problem working here, preparing the food to be sold. But she wasn't so sure about tending the counter and the cash register.

"Here's a schedule for the time I'll be gone." Rusty slapped a sheet of paper down on the worktable. "Brenna will be here every day for you except one. She's agreed to do some extra hours that week. Now, let me walk you through what I do every morning."

Shelley followed him around, paying close attention. There was so much to remember that she began scrawling notes on the back of the employee schedule. By the time Rusty paused and said, "Okay, it's time to open," her mind whirled.

"Can I come back another time and go over this again?"

"Sure," Rusty said. "Besides, we haven't talked about the closing routine yet. The cleanup and the cashing out, all of that. Oh, and the bank deposits. Best to do that every afternoon when it's slower in here."

Shelley gulped. "Right. Thanks—I'll come back one afternoon to go over all that."

She made her escape out the back door and drove toward home. She had three dozen boxed giant Valentine cookies at home she had to mail. But first she needed to see Dan off and get Aiden and Hailey to school. Then she could think about getting over to the post office. How would she ever cope the week Rusty was gone and she had to be at the Cove ready for early-bird coffee customers by 6:00 AM?

★ ★ ★

Margaret closed the notebook containing her menu and to-do list for the Valentine dinner she was preparing. Allan was coming to tend the gallery for her while she went to the grocery store, and she didn't want him to see that.

The lengthy list of ingredients was somewhat daunting—she'd never even heard of a couple of the items she needed for her dinner preparations. But she was willing to learn.

She hadn't been able to come up with an explanation for Allan as to why she wanted to do the grocery shopping herself this week. He would find that extremely odd, since she avoided the supermarket as much as possible. Instead, she'd just told him she needed to do some shopping for her Valentine surprise, and he hadn't asked any questions. He really was a prince.

Thank heaven she kept shorter hours at the gallery in winter. Otherwise, she'd never be able to juggle this surprise along with her tai chi classes, ballroom dancing, and her business.

Allan arrived punctually, to keep the shop open for its last two hours of the day before heading to the community center to pick up Adelaide, and Margaret set off for the store in Willow Corners. She had to enlist the help of a stock boy in finding a couple of items, but to her relief, she arrived home before Allan and Adelaide did.

Anything that didn't need refrigeration, she stowed in a box on her side of the closet, back behind the skirts of her longest dresses. Those that had to be kept cool, she put in two plastic grocery sacks. Which of her neighbors could she impose on with the smallest impact? She hated to disturb Diane, in case she wasn't feeling well. Shelley's refrigerator was probably full of baking ingredients. She grabbed the sacks and dashed over to the Wheelands' house.

Mr. Wheeland came to the door.

"Hi," Margaret said with a sheepish smile. "I should have asked you earlier, but I wondered if you have any extra room in your fridge. I'm making a surprise dinner for Allan on Thursday, and I don't want him to know."

"I think we can manage that," Mr. Wheeland said jovially. "Come right in. We'll just have to be sure to mark your bags, or Mrs. Peabody might use your groceries to make our lunch."

At last the sour cream, meat, flavored creamer, and fresh produce were stored away, and Margaret thanked her neighbor profusely.

"No problem," he said. "I expect you'll be over Thursday morning to get everything?"

"Yes, I will. I'm taking the afternoon off to prepare the meal."

"I'm sure it will be scrumptious," he said as they walked out to the hall.

The front door opened, and Beverly came in. "Oh, Margaret! Hello."

Margaret smiled. "Hi. Your father's helping me out with a little secret. I'll let him explain. Allan will be home any minute, and I need to get back."

* * *

Beverly stood on the front porch waving as Margaret left. Allan's car rolled down the street just as Margaret reached their driveway. Poor Margaret! She would probably be flustered in her efforts to explain where she'd been. And Allan was so easygoing that it wouldn't matter.

The town council meeting was scheduled for seven o'clock, so Beverly went back inside to see about supper.

She would have an early meal with her father and then go over her notes and change for the meeting.

She was a little nervous going into the meeting, but the preliminaries went smoothly. Once the council president recognized her during the "new business" session and she stood to address the council, she felt more at ease. She was used to presenting facts and figures.

Her handout of suggested places where they could realign funds kept everyone quiet for a few minutes as they read her recommendations. Beverly kept her eye on treasurer Lionel Riley. His frown grew deeper and deeper. She decided it would be better to jump in with an upbeat spin than to wait for him to object to something she'd written.

"I believe we can make some small but effective changes in our spending this year," she said. "Mr. Riley always does a great job in preparing the budget, and I thought we might discuss a few things before he begins that process. You all know that the biggest share of our annual budget goes to the school district. Once that's approved, we can't change it. But we *can* change the other local allocations."

"You think we need to spend that much on summer roads this year?" Mr. Riley asked, staring down at the paper in his hand.

Beverly nodded soberly. "Since I've been in office, I've had complaints about some of our roads. I've talked to our road commissioner about specific stretches that he agrees need resurfacing. The town has tried to stay on a ten-year paving schedule, but it seems we haven't resurfaced a few of

our outlying roads in more than fifteen years. And they need
it badly."

"We had to redo the bridge last year," Jules Benton said,
shaking his head. "That took most of the money."

"I understand," Beverly told him. "That was an emergency.
Perhaps it's time to think about starting a capital fund for
unforeseen expenses."

"And how do you plan to finance all this paving?"
Mr. Riley asked.

"People won't like it if we raise their property taxes,"
Martha Goodman, a new council member, said.

"That's true," Beverly said, smiling at her. "I'm asking
for about half again as much as we budgeted for this last
year. I've found a few spots where we can shave off some
spending. Look at the bottom half of the sheet. Last year,
the town donated almost three thousand dollars to third-
party organizations outside Marble Cove."

"Do our people use these services?" Mrs. Goodman
asked.

"That's an excellent question," Beverly said. "If Marble
Cove people are helped by them, perhaps we should continue
to donate. But I'd like to see some hard figures from them,
showing how our residents have benefited."

"It's still not enough to pay for all the paving you want to
do," said Mr. Riley.

"Did you read all the way to the bottom?" asked Terry
Dwiggins, another new member of the council. Owner of
a landscaping business, he was so handsome that Beverly

wondered whether some of the women found him a distraction.

"Thank you," she said with a nod to Mr. Dwiggins. "I've also suggested some other cuts we can make."

Beverly looked around at the six council members. All were studying the paper she'd distributed.

"If we cut a little from the other budget items noted, I think we could have some pretty good-looking roads by fall, without raising the tax rate." She smiled at the treasurer. "Mr. Riley, I'm requesting that you look at these suggestions and see if you find them reasonable. Or maybe you can see other places I've missed where we can save some dollars."

Mr. Riley grunted and stuck his paper into a folder, signaling that he was done looking at it for now.

"Thank you all for listening," Beverly said. "And I'd be happy to meet privately with Mr. Riley or any of you who have concerns."

Jules Benton shrugged, his gavel in his hand. "And what do you wish us to do now, Mayor?"

"Just think about it," Beverly said. "If you disagree with the points I've made, that's fine. We should have some open discussion before the budget is finalized. I'm sure Mr. Riley would like to hear your comments too. We all want the same thing—to run the town efficiently, without wasting the people's money."

"Amen to that," Harry Vogel, manager of the local grocery store, said.

"All right," said Mr. Benton, "Is there any more new business?"

Beverly sat down, her heart pounding. Mr. Riley hadn't actually opposed her, but she wondered if he was angry and felt she had undermined his past work on the budget. She hoped he would want to work with her.

When the meeting ended, the people who had come to listen filed out. Martha Goodman came over to speak to Beverly.

"You made some good points, Mayor. But I came on this board hoping to make a difference in the town, and specifically to help Marble Cove develop and draw in new businesses and new jobs."

"I'm glad to hear it," Beverly said. "We could use a boost in our economy. But a lot of people are adamant about their taxes too. The town hasn't gone hog wild in past spending. I'd just like to see it more focused—on things that directly benefit our residents."

"Well, you've inspired me to get out last year's budget and give it a hard look."

"Good! Come see me when you've done that and we'll talk."

Beverly wondered if Martha would line up as a staunch supporter of Dennis Calder's new plans for the train station. She picked up her briefcase and glanced down the table. Lionel Riley was scowling at her.

★ ★ ★

Diane was up early on Wednesday and took Rocky out for a walk before breakfast. She was brewing tea and heating some oatmeal when Beverly arrived on her doorstep.

"Hi. Just thought I'd check in and see if you needed any help this morning," Beverly said.

"Thanks, but I think everything's under control."

Beverly smiled. "Feeling better?"

"Yes. Rocky and I have been out already this morning. I hope to do some writing today."

"Good. I've got some work to do at home myself, and then I'll probably go to the town office for a few hours this afternoon," Beverly said.

"Can you sit for a few minutes?" Diane asked. "I've got a pot of tea ready."

"All right." Beverly came in and removed her coat and gloves.

Diane poured out the tea into bone china cups with cheerful floral designs—bachelor's buttons and daffodils.

"So Jeff's coming tomorrow to take you out," she said as she sat down across from Beverly.

"I can't wait to see him." Beverly smiled with a little shrug, as though she were self-conscious. "Does that sound juvenile?"

"Not at all," Diane assured her.

"How about you? You're not going out at all?"

"I think Valentine's Day is overrated." Diane immediately felt remorse at her choice of words. "I'm sorry. I know it will be meaningful for you and Jeff, but since I don't have anyone special right now, it's really more stressful than otherwise."

"Have you been thinking about Eric?" Beverly asked.

Her insight surprised Diane. "A little."

"It's all right to miss him, you know."

"Oh yes. And I'm truly not feeling guilty anymore." Diane chuckled. "I really thought I had completely worked through the issue of widowhood, but sometimes it still hits me, it's true."

"It took me a long time." Beverly sipped her tea, and they sat in silence for a moment. Their experiences were very different, and each had found her own comfortable way of dealing with the harsh reality.

"Eric was so special. It's hard for me not to wonder if any other man could measure up to him. But that's not fair to guys like Leo." She shrugged. "I don't know, maybe this sadness has nothing to do with Eric. Maybe I'm just down because I hate having anyone feel bad toward me."

"You don't think Leo holds it against you for turning down a date, do you?" Beverly asked.

"Probably not. But Margaret pointed something out to me a week or two ago. She says I love to nurture people, and she's right. That's what makes me feel complete and adequate. If I do something that upsets another person, I drag around for days, even if I know that I did the right thing."

"I don't think that's unusual. Everyone wants the people around her to love her and think she's wonderful. I know I do—

but I seldom feel that it's true." Beverly held up a hand. "Now, don't try to convince me otherwise, that's not my point. I'm just saying, it's natural not to want Leo to think badly of you."

"Okay." Diane lifted her cup and sipped the fragrant tea. "You know, I do have *some* feelings for Leo."

"Beyond friendship?"

"I don't know. That's the problem. I'm not sure if they're rest-of-my-life feelings. And I don't want to make any decisions I'll regret while I'm not feeling my best physically."

"I can see the sense of that." Beverly set her cup down on the saucer. "You could put it to Leo just like that. He ought to understand. Then leave it open for further discussion. When you're finished with treatment and feel like yourself again, you might decide that you want to step up the relationship. Don't slam the door completely on it."

"You're right. I should tell him that." Diane gave a rueful little laugh. "If I ever get a chance. I may have driven him away for good."

"Don't say that. I don't think Leo's that fragile." Beverly glanced up at the kitchen clock. "Well, I hate to say it, but I'd better get home and get some work done. Call me if you need anything, okay?"

"I will, thanks." Diane walked with her to the door. "And thanks for the good advice."

★ ★ ★

Margaret closed the gallery an hour early on Wednesday afternoon. Allan had driven to Augusta to pick out some wood for the inlaid tables he was working on. It was the perfect time for her to get a few things done in preparation for tomorrow's surprise.

Unfortunately, most of the work would have to be done the day of the dinner. Margaret couldn't see how she could open the gallery on Valentine's Day and still have time to cook all of the complicated recipes she had selected. She decided she would have to tell Allan what she was up to—or at least that she would be doing something special all day. She would ban him from the kitchen. With his new batch of wood on hand, he'd probably be happy to spend most of the day in his workshop. Or perhaps he'd even open the gallery for the morning hours. One way or another, she'd keep him away while she got everything ready.

For now, she would have to be content with putting together the dried-flower centerpiece, organizing the ingredients for tomorrow's cooking marathon, and making the crab puff appetizers. She thought it would be all right to make those a day ahead and put them in the back of the fridge in an airtight container. Of course, she'd have to mark it "Don't Peek," or Allan would see the container and know someone else put it there. He'd be curious and look.

She had never worked with phyllo dough before, and she wasn't sure she was doing it right. At last she had the crab puffs put together, and she spaced them evenly on a cookie sheet. She opened the oven to slide them in and realized she had forgotten to turn it on. With a sigh, she fiddled with the controls. What would she say if Allan came home and the puffs were still in the oven? She cleaned up while the oven heated, trying to get rid of all traces of her activity in Allan's domain. She hoped fervently that the appetizers would be baked and out of sight before he came home.

It wasn't Allan, but their daughter Adelaide who burst through the kitchen door a few minutes later.

"Mom! What are you doing here? I thought you were at the gallery."

Margaret smiled at Adelaide's understandable confusion. "I came home early to fix a surprise for your father."

"A surprise?" Adelaide loved surprises. Her eyes lit up.

"That's right, so you can't tell him anything about this, okay?"

"Okay."

Margaret frowned. "How did you get home?" She glanced at her watch. "I was going to pick you up at the community center at five." Adelaide occasionally helped Penny Tyler as a way to practice the skills she was learning in her college classes.

"We finished early today, and Penny dropped me off."

"Oh. That was nice of her."

Adelaide's nose crinkled. "What's that smell?"

Margaret whirled toward the stove. Smoke seeped out along the top of the oven door. "Oh no!" She grabbed a pot holder and opened the oven. The crab puffs looked like hard little sienna-colored nuggets and gave off an acrid odor. She snatched the pan out and put it on top of the stove. "They're ruined!"

Adelaide stared at them. "What were they? Cookies?"

"No. Appetizers. Quick!" Margaret ran to the window and peeked out. There was no sign of Allan yet. "Turn on the fan over the oven, and then go turn on the one in the bathroom. I'm going to open the doors for a few minutes. Maybe we can get this smell out of here before Dad gets home."

In the next five minutes, they ventilated by every means they could think of and sprayed air sanitizer in the kitchen. Margaret vaguely recalled hearing that unpleasant kitchen smells could be overpowered by more pleasant ones. She put a pan of water on to heat and poured a couple of capfuls of vanilla into it.

In a flash of brilliance, she picked up the phone and called the gallery. When Allan answered, she huffed out a breath in relief. "Hi, sweetheart. I'm so glad I caught you."

"I'll probably be another ten or fifteen minutes," he said in a low voice. "I'm packaging up a painting for a late customer."

From his tone, Margaret gathered that the customer was still in the store, though it was nearly ten past five.

"That's fine," she said, "but could you pick up some…uh, some milk before you come home?"

"Milk? I thought we had a new gallon."

"Oh. Do we?" She gritted her teeth and swung the refrigerator door open. "So we do. How about orange juice?"

"We need orange juice?"

As she spoke, Margaret pulled open the freezer door to make sure there wasn't any frozen concentrate in there.

"It looks like it. Would you mind?"

Allan hesitated. "No, that's fine. I'll see you later."

"Okay," Margaret said to Adelaide as she hung up. "We've got at least twenty minutes, maybe thirty. What else can we do?"

"Burn some toast?" Adelaide suggested.

Margaret laughed. "That might camouflage the smell, but I think the vanilla's starting to work, and it's much nicer. Let's keep fanning and see if we can't clear out the rest of the smoke before he gets home."

"Okay." Adelaide picked up a newspaper and waved it in the air over her head, where a few wisps of smoke still lingered near the ceiling.

"And remember," Margaret told her, "not a word about my cooking."

Chapter Seven

Dan pushed back from the breakfast table and pulled on his jacket.

"You all set for today, Shell?"

"Yes, Emma and I are going to the bank right after we drop off Hailey and Aiden at school." Shelley smiled, thinking of the profits she had made on her marathon cookie baking this week.

"Don't forget about tonight." Dan wiggled his eyebrows. His attempt at a mysterious smile crooked to one side, and she laughed.

"I'll be ready. I can hardly wait."

They rarely had a night out together, let alone one that called for high heels and a fancy dress. Shelley intended to make the most of the evening.

"You got a sitter, right?" she asked as he reached for his lunch box.

Dan froze with his hand in midair. "Oh man!" He turned toward her, his teeth clenched. "I'm sorry, Shelley. I forgot."

Shelley bit back an angry retort. Dan had promised her two things—a dinner reservation and a babysitter. She was bitterly disappointed, but she didn't want to ruin the atmosphere for their date by getting upset now.

Hailey looked up from her French toast and lifted her fork into the air. "We'd be okay for a couple of hours, Aunt Shelley."

"Oh, I don't think so, honey. I know you're great with the kids, but at night..." She looked at Dan. No way would she leave Aiden and Emma alone with a nine-year-old.

Dan walked over and kissed her. "I'll try and think of someone, but I've got to run. I'm really sorry. If not tonight, I can move our reservation to Saturday."

"Okay."

He went out the door, and his truck's engine started.

"I don't see why we need a sitter," Hailey said. "Girls my age babysit all the time."

Shelley didn't want to get into a lengthy discussion. Maybe in Hailey's old neighborhood that was true. She smiled and said, "I'll try to get someone you guys like." She thought of her mother-in-law, but she didn't like to call on Frances too often. Maybe one of her friends at church would have some ideas.

She glanced at the clock. "Get your coats on, guys. We need to get going."

Hailey carried her dishes to the sink.

Aiden hopped down from his chair and picked up his bowl and spoon. "Where's my pack, Mom?"

A few harried minutes followed as they gathered school bags and lunches and got bundled up for the cold.

"Here!" Shelley thrust Hailey's lunch bag into her hand, and they all dashed out the door. Prize followed them as far as she could, barking. "Hush!" Shelley closed the door firmly and checked to be sure it was locked. When all of the children were buckled into their seats in the car, she got behind the wheel. Some mornings she felt like a robot whose timing belt needed adjusting.

When she and Emma returned home half an hour later, Shelley removed Emma's snowsuit and put her in her booster seat. She gave her a few pieces of cereal and two small toys.

"Okay, sweetie, you can play for a minute. Mommy's got to make a phone call or two."

Twenty minutes later, she admitted defeat. No babysitters were available that night in Marble Cove. Even Frances and Ralph were going out with a couple of friends. Shelley had extracted a promise for Saturday night, if needed, from a high school girl whose parents wouldn't let her babysit on school nights. Shelley called her number again.

"Jennie's gone to school, but I'll tell her," the girl's mother said.

"Thanks very much." Shelley hung up with a sigh. It was the best she could do. So much for her big night out.

She sat in silence for a moment and then whispered, "Well, Lord, You're going to have to help me. I need an attitude adjustment. Let me somehow get as excited about Saturday as I was about tonight."

Emma had begun to fuss and wriggle in her seat. Shelley unstrapped her and set her down on the floor. "There you go."

Emma toddled over to Prize and patted the little dog. Prize yipped and licked her face.

Shelley began transferring all of the dirty dishes into the dishwasher. Emma had settled on the floor with one of Aiden's toy trucks, so she wiped off the table. When she had finished, she glanced around the kitchen, then scooped Emma up off the floor, truck and all.

"All right, time for baking. Mommy's got more work to do."

★ ★ ★

Beverly heard Jeff arrive, but she wasn't quite ready. He'd e-mailed to ask if she was up to a drive to Camden tonight. A restaurant on the harbor would be a nice change, but they'd have a bit of a drive, and first they needed to stop by Reverend Locke's house to discuss reserving the church for their wedding.

She listened to be sure her father opened the door for him and then went back into the bathroom to put the finishing touches on her makeup. Tonight should be a wonderful evening. She and Jeff had so much to talk about.

She picked up her brush for one final run through her hair and froze. What was that sound?

It came again, and her heart lurched. Unless she was mistaken, that was a dog barking. A dog, inside the house. What on earth was going on?

She went to her bedroom, grabbed her purse, and hurried down the stairs. The hallway below was now empty, so she followed the sound of voices to the library. Her father sat in his recliner, cuddling a wriggling, fluffy little dog. Jeff hovered nearby, beaming.

"...and he's so alert," her father was saying.

She paused in the doorway. "Hi, Jeff. What's this?"

He grinned at her, and for just a moment she thrilled at the knowledge of her position. She was going to marry the finest, most handsome man on earth. And then he opened his mouth.

"It's my gift to you, sweetheart. Happy Valentine's Day."

Beverly gulped. "A dog?"

"A puppy," her father corrected.

"He's old enough to be on his own," Jeff assured her. "Twelve weeks. He's a schnoodle."

"Isn't that cute?" her father asked as the gray puppy licked his face.

"A...did you say schnoodle?" Beverly asked weakly. How could Jeff not know that she disliked dogs?

"Part schnauzer, part poodle," Jeff said. "He's really intelligent. I know he'll train easily. I thought you and your dad would like having a companion, and when I come to visit, I can play with him too. When we have our own place..." He watched her expectantly.

Beverly managed a smile. "I see." She made herself step forward and pat the puppy's head. It wiggled beneath her hand as the pup squirmed to see who touched him. Beverly caught a breath and pulled her hand away. "Lively, isn't he?"

"Oh yeah, he's in great health," Jeff said. "I made sure he had the first round of puppy shots. Of course, you'll want to have him fixed when he's a little older..."

Later, she couldn't remember anything Jeff said after that. All she knew was that he helped her put on her coat, and they left the house with her father calling assurances that all would be fine while they enjoyed their evening.

"I absolutely fell in love with that pup the minute I saw him," Jeff said as he turned in the direction of Reverend Locke's house.

It was all falling into place. Beverly couldn't help but notice the thrill in his voice and the spark in his eyes when he talked about that scrappy little puppy.

She smiled at him. "I'm guessing you always wanted a dog when you were a kid."

"Well, yeah. What boy doesn't?"

She nodded. "Why didn't you get a dog before now?"

"I didn't have a good place for one, and I'm away so much...But this will be great, don't you think?"

She avoided a direct answer to the question. "I'm sure we'll have some...memorable times with the puppy."

"For sure. And when he's bigger, he can go out with you when you jog. And your dad really seemed to like him."

"Yes, he did, didn't he?"

Jeff pulled into the driveway and parked behind the minister's dark sedan. He hopped out and rounded the SUV to open Beverly's door.

"I hope you brought your schedule," she said softly as they walked up to the porch hand in hand.

Jeff patted his chest. "Right here. Good thing you mentioned it, though."

She pushed the doorbell, and Reverend Locke opened the door almost at once.

"Hello! Come right in. Nice to see you both!" He shook Jeff's hand enthusiastically. "Let me take your coats. May I offer you some coffee?"

Jeff shot Beverly a questioning look.

"None for me, thanks," she said. "We're going on to Camden for dinner this evening, so I don't expect we'll be here long. We just need to confirm a date for the church— and your services too, of course, if you're willing."

"I'd be honored to perform the wedding. Thank you for asking me." Reverend Locke led them into his living room and gestured toward the avocado tweed sofa.

Beverly and Jeff sat down together, and the minister took a seat in his leather recliner. Beverly had gotten used to the reverend's bachelor décor, but Jeff seemed quite interested in the prints of sailing ships that hung on the stark off-white walls.

"We hoped to finalize the date tonight if we can." Beverly took her day planner from her purse. "Do you think a May wedding is feasible at Old First?"

"May? *Hmm.*" Reverend Locke pushed his glasses up on his nose. "The repairs aren't finished yet. The roof is done, of course, but there's a bit more to be done inside."

"I thought the fire damage was all taken care of," Jeff said.

"Most of it is, thanks to Beverly and her friends and the discovery they made that helped finance the work." Reverend Locke looked at her benevolently.

Beverly smiled back. She felt very good about the way she, Diane, Margaret, and Shelley had found a way to meet the church's dire need. "Looking back on it now, I know God was with us every step of the way."

"Amen," Reverend Locke said softly. "Well, let's see, the work should be done by mid-May at the latest. And the women's group is having a mother-daughter tea at the church the Saturday before Mother's Day."

"Oh, we won't want to get married that weekend," Beverly said quickly. Too many people would have other plans for the holiday.

"How about the Saturday after?" Reverend Locke stood and walked to a wall calendar that bore a scenic view of the ocean. He lifted three leaves until the month of May showed. "That would be the eighteenth."

A soft, warm feeling swept over Beverly. May eighteenth. Would that be her wedding day? She turned to Jeff. "What do you say? Is the eighteenth all right?"

"Oh, uh…" Jeff pulled out his smartphone and scrolled through it. "Sorry. I'm scheduled to go to Prince Edward Island that week."

"Oh." Beverly realized suddenly that they needed not only a free day for the wedding, but time for the honeymoon as well. "What other assignments do you have coming up?"

"Well, there's one May twenty-third and twenty-fourth. I'm shooting some white-water rafting on the Kennebec."

"But you have the Saturday free?" Reverend Locke asked. "The twenty-fifth?"

"Yes, but if anything happened and I was delayed..." Jeff cast an anxious glance at Beverly. "I wouldn't want to take a chance on missing the rehearsal or anything like that."

Beverly swallowed hard against the lump forming in her throat. Was Jeff's schedule too busy for him to get married?

"Well, that puts us into June, assuming you want a Saturday." The reverend turned another page on the calendar.

Jeff looked down at his. "Yeah, that would work for me. I don't have any assignments in the week leading up to the first, and I've got three weeks free afterward, before that Costa Rica job I was telling you about." He gazed soberly at Beverly. "I still hope you'll be able to go with me on that one."

Beverly's world righted itself. "We'll talk about that later. It would be wonderful if we can work it out, but right now let's settle the wedding date."

Jeff smiled sheepishly. "I guess I blocked out June instead of May. Sorry."

"No, it's okay," she said. "If the church is free June first, let's do that. Just keep those weeks afterward open, you hear me?"

"I hear you," Jeff said.

"And so do I," Reverend Locke said heartily. "I'm writing it on the calendar as we speak, so it's now official."

They left a few minutes later. To Beverly, having the date fixed was a huge relief. Her lists and plans would have a focus now.

"So," Jeff said as they glided toward Camden, "June 1." He smiled at her. "Big changes coming."

"Yes." That made her think of the puppy. "I ought to call Father and see how he's making out."

"I'm sure he's fine."

"I'll feel better if I call." She took out her phone, and Jeff said no more. Her father didn't answer until the phone had rung four times, and she felt a bit guilty. She'd probably gotten him up out of his recliner.

"Hello."

She tried to read something into his voice, but she couldn't. "Father, it's me. How's the puppy doing?"

"Fine," he said. "He's been sniffing around and getting to know the place. We'll have to get him a few toys. I gave him an old sock."

"Oh." Beverly wasn't sure how to respond to that. She couldn't quite picture the tousle-haired little dog playing with a sock.

"Oh, and I put some papers down in the kitchen," her father said.

"Papers? Oh. Just a second." She took the phone away from her ear and said to Jeff, "Is that dog house-trained?"

"I'm not sure. He's probably learning."

"Well, I don't want Father taking him outside tonight."

"I brought a leash," Jeff reminded her.

"Yes, but Father could fall."

Jeff grimaced. "Sorry. I should have thought of that before we left him."

"We couldn't very well bring him and leave him in the car," Beverly said, a bit curtly. She didn't want to get into an argument over the dog, but at the moment she wasn't very pleased about this new wrinkle.

"I guess you'll have to resort to the newspapers," she said into the phone. "I'm sorry, Father. We're only about halfway to Camden. Do you want us to come home?"

"No, no." Her father sounded almost jovial now. "Don't worry about us."

"You won't take him out, will you? It's very cold out."

"We'll be fine," he said again. "Now, enjoy yourselves."

She gulped. "I'll try." She put the phone away and looked bleakly at Jeff.

"I'll take the puppy out as soon as we get back," Jeff said.

"Thank you. I hope he holds out that long, but it will be quite a stretch for a baby, won't it?"

"Probably. I'm sorry—but your father's right to use newspapers. Sounds like he has things under control. And within a few days, you'll have him trained and used to your routine."

"Right."

* * *

Margaret spent four hours preparing her special dinner for Allan. Adelaide was spending the evening with her friends at a group home in town, and Margaret wished belatedly that she had enlisted her help. Getting everything to turn out well at the same time became an insurmountable challenge.

In order to get Allan out of the way, she'd had to break down and tell him she was fixing a surprise. He had smiled indulgently and offered to keep the gallery open for her until five. After closing, he had called to say he would run an errand or two, and she'd thanked him profusely. He was such a dear, but by then she was having serious doubts about her romantic gourmet dinner.

She didn't have time to redo the appetizers she had ruined the day before. When she took out the recipe for the mozzarella-and-asparagus-stuffed chicken breasts, she realized that she hadn't yet retrieved the chicken and other items from the Wheelands' refrigerator. A quick trip up the street fixed that, except that the chicken was frozen rock-solid.

"Don't panic," she told herself. "That's what we have microwave ovens for." She peeled the block of frozen chicken off the Styrofoam tray and put it in the microwave in a glass casserole dish. She had no idea how long it would take to thaw, so she decided to let it run while she peeled the potatoes and started the dessert.

When she finally thought to check on the chicken, it was not only thawed, but half cooked. The edges looked done and felt slightly rubbery, but the middle was still raw. Had she used the wrong setting? Normally, she only turned to the microwave to heat a cup of tea water or a dish of leftovers.

She sighed and gazed at the casserole dish. She would have to let the chicken cool off before she could handle it. The recipe called for slicing and pounding.

She looked at the clock. She'd been a fool to think she could do this. Before she could go into a rant against herself, the pan of potatoes began to boil over, sending hot water over the entire top of the stove.

At ten minutes to seven, the phone rang. She walked over to answer it with wooden legs.

"Hello, sweetheart," Allan said.

"Where are you?" Margaret tried to keep her voice even, but it trembled treacherously.

"Sitting in the driveway. Do you need more time?"

Margaret looked around at the disaster she had created in the last four hours.

"*Nooo.* You may as well come in. It's not going to get any better."

"All right, see you in a sec."

She stood still, her head drooping. How could she have ruined so many dishes in one swoop? The chicken was the worst disaster—it was inedible. The salad dressing looked gray, and the soup had stuck on and scorched. Even the herbed mashed potatoes were ruined. She'd misread the amount of garlic, and the spuds were now so pungent they wouldn't have to worry about vampires coming around for years.

Allan pushed the kitchen door open and entered grinning, holding an armful of hothouse flowers.

"Happy Valentine's Day, sweetheart."

Margaret burst into tears.

Allan's nose wrinkled. He laid the flowers on the counter and took her into his arms. "There now, it can't be that bad."

"Worse," she choked.

He stroked her back for a moment, then said calmly, "What can I do to help?"

"Nothing. It's all ruined."

He held her close. "Would this be a good time to suggest we go out to dinner?"

Margaret sighed. "I don't know what else we can do at this point, unless you want to make scrambled eggs."

"Why don't you go change your clothes, and I'll do a little cleaning up here." As he spoke, Allan turned off the oven and a burner and switched on the fan.

She sniffed. "Thank you. But I *will* learn to cook, Allan. I *have* to now."

"If you want to. But you don't need to think about it tonight. Go on. I'll call the Landmark and see if they can squeeze us in."

Margaret appreciated his sweet, even temper. She really did, but sometimes it made her feel like a horrible failure in comparison. Why couldn't she be more like Allan? You'd think, after all these years together, that some of his serenity and efficiency would have rubbed off on her.

CHAPTER EIGHT

Beverly's nerves were taut by the time they got back to Newport Avenue. They'd been gone nearly four hours—plenty of time for several canine disasters. She was afraid she'd ruined the ambiance at dinner by fretting about her father and that puppy. She'd tried to keep up with everything Jeff said about his job and the wedding and the possible jaunt to Costa Rica in late June, but her thoughts had kept sliding back home.

She didn't wait for him to open her car door, but hopped out and dashed up the front steps. The door was locked, and instead of ringing for her father to let them in, she had her key out and opened the door before Jeff had reached the porch.

Her father was coming into the entry. "I thought I heard you drive in. Awfully early, aren't you?"

Beverly stopped short and pulled in a deep breath. "Is everything all right?"

"Well, that depends on what you mean by 'all right.' We both survived the evening, and we even had fun playing tug-of-war with the sock. But I'm afraid our little friend did have an accident."

The puppy came barreling out of the dining room and careered toward them, yapping at the top of his lungs. Behind her, Jeff laughed and shut the door.

"Come here, fella." He stepped past Beverly and knelt to greet the puppy. "There, did you miss us?" He ruffled the schnoodle's fluffy head and stroked his back, all the way to the pup's wriggling tail.

"Where did he do it?" Beverly demanded as she removed her coat and gloves.

"Under the dining table," her father said. "I was just about to clean it up."

"You'll do no such thing!" The idea of him crawling around under there to clean a smelly mess appalled her.

Her father smiled sheepishly. "Guess I was hoping to have it done before you saw it."

"I'll take care of it," Jeff said.

"No, you take him outside and let him romp," Beverly said grimly. "I want him all tired out before we settle down for the night. Otherwise he'll probably keep us awake to all hours."

Half an hour later, things had calmed down. Beverly had cleaned the dining room floor and was able to give thanks that it hadn't been on the carpet in the living room or her father's library. Jeff had delighted in giving the pup some exercise, and he let the little rascal fall asleep on his lap while he stroked it lovingly. She fixed decaf coffee and took the tray into the living room.

"You just need to be consistent in training him," Jeff said confidently, running his hand over the curve of the puppy's head. "As soon as he knows that you'll take him outside regularly, he'll always do it there."

She sighed. Already it was too late to try to get out of this. She was now a dog owner, like it or not.

"Are you driving back to Portland tonight?" her father asked Jeff.

"No, I decided to stay at the Landmark. I'll go home tomorrow and do laundry and repack my suitcase. I head out for Texas tomorrow."

"That'll be quite a change in climate," Father said.

"Yes, I'm shooting pictures of birds along the Rio Grande. Should be fun."

"Send us some warm weather."

Jeff laughed and continued to pat the puppy. He smiled at Beverly. "It'll be great coming home to you and this little guy when I'm finished."

Beverly couldn't bring herself to answer that cheerfully, so she smiled and sipped her coffee.

★ ★ ★

Diane showered early and put on her warm pajamas, fuzzy slipper socks, and robe. She curled up on the sofa near the stone fireplace with a popular mystery author's newest book. Rocky lay down on the rug within patting range. The book started out with a bang, and Diane read avidly, stopping occasionally to gaze into the flames and think how masterfully the plot was drawing her along.

She was about to begin a new chapter when her phone rang. She rose and hurried to get it, her legs a little wobbly from having sat so long.

"Hi, Diane. It's Allan Hoskins."

"Well, hi, Allan." Diane was startled to hear his voice. Allan almost never called her, but his even tone kept her from becoming alarmed.

"Margaret and I are going out," he said. "We're just going over to the Landmark to get some dinner—sort of a last-minute thing. Would you like to join us?"

Diane smiled. How sweet of Margaret to think of her sitting home alone tonight. Even if she was keen on going out, she wouldn't want to spoil the couple's Valentine evening together. "Thanks awfully, but I'm already in my pj's and cozy by the fire. I think I'm too lazy to dress up again."

"Oh well..." Allan paused, then said brightly. "How about dessert then? We can get it 'to go' and bring it over to your place and share it with you. What do you say?"

He seemed genuinely eager to include her in the fun. Diane looked down at her fluffy slipper socks and laughed. "If you don't mind the hostess wearing a frumpy bathrobe, come on over. I'll make the coffee."

"Great. We'll see you later. Now don't you dare change or do any housework."

"Agreed." She hung up and looked over at Rocky, who had barely stirred. "Well, boy, it looks like we're having company tonight. At least the place isn't too messy. I'd better keep the fire going, though. The dust won't show by firelight."

A few minutes later, she received another phone call, this time from her son Justin who was making a career of the army. Delighted as always to hear from him, Diane chatted for a few minutes and assured him that she was taking it easy and making progress in her recovery.

"Have you talked to Jessica lately?" Justin asked.

"Monday, I think," Diane said.

"She seemed a little blue the last time I talked to her. Do you think everything's okay with her and Martin?"

Diane frowned. "I hope so. She did tell me he'd seemed a little distant when it came to making plans for the wedding."

"*Hmm*. I hope she's all right. She didn't say anything specific to me," Justin said, "but I got the feeling things were a little off-kilter."

Diane had been praying for Jessica and Martin's relationship daily, and had assumed that if the situation got worse, Jessica would tell her. Now she wondered if her daughter needed some encouragement.

"I'll definitely talk to her this weekend," she promised.

"Okay, thanks," Justin said. "She'd tell you stuff she probably wouldn't tell me."

Half an hour after they hung up, Allan and Margaret arrived. Rocky jumped up when they drove in and he ran to the door, barking.

"Hush, you." Diane walked quickly to the door and frowned down at him, pointing to his bed. "Lie down."

Rocky slunk to the bed, turned around, and eased down on the cushion.

"Good boy." Diane opened the door and let the Hoskinses in.

Margaret gave her a big hug. "I think you had the right idea, staying in. It's cold out there!"

Diane laughed and took their coats. Allan set the white box with the dessert on the kitchen table.

"Thank you! What did you bring?" Diane asked. "I set out plates and forks."

"It's cheesecake." Allan opened the box, disclosing three generous slices of creamy cheesecake with a splash of clear, red sauce on each, garnished with a swirl of dark chocolate and one plump, perfect raspberry.

"Ooh, that looks too pretty to eat," Diane said.

"That never stopped me," Margaret told her with a laugh.

They fixed their plates and mugs of coffee and retreated to the living room.

Margaret and Allan entertained Diane with tales of their ballroom-dancing classes.

"Margaret is quite good at the fox-trot," Allan said.

"Yes, and I can waltz," Margaret added. "But those Latin dances—forget it."

Diane laughed. "I'm sure I'd be horrible at those."

"You ought to give it a try," Allan said. "I think we're learning the quickstep next time."

"Thanks, but I don't think I'm ready to do much quickstepping."

Margaret smiled. "Maybe in a few weeks, if you can think of someone who might like to be your partner."

Diane wondered if this was a hint about Leo. "I don't think so."

Margaret smiled. "That's okay. I don't think we told you how we decided to go out to eat tonight, did we?"

Allan eyed her in surprise. "I wasn't sure you wanted to broadcast it. There's nothing to be ashamed of, but I didn't say anything."

"What happened?" Diane looked from one to the other of them.

Margaret laughed and shook her head. "It was my fault. You remember how I was going to make this big, romantic dinner for Allan. I'd been planning for weeks and finding recipes and hiding the food over at the Wheelands'. And then...well, let's just say it didn't turn out very well."

"I'm sorry," Diane said as she lifted the first bite of the cheesecake to her mouth. "Oh, this is good."

Margaret and Allan began to eat too, and all agreed that the cheesecake was a worthy ending to the day.

After a few bites, Margaret sighed, and Diane knew she was still thinking about her cooking fiasco. "It wouldn't have been so bad, except for wasting all that food, of course, but I really wanted to do something special for Valentine's Day. And it turned out that Allan, as usual, ended up doing something for me instead. He brought me flowers and took me out of the messy kitchen I'd created." She looked at him with a loving smile. "You're still my hero."

Allan leaned over and kissed her lightly. "All culinary problems aside, I had a very good time this evening. We even got to show off our fox-trot at the Landmark tonight."

"Really?" Diane asked. "They had dancing?"

"Yes, Victoria hired a band for the evening. It was very nice." Margaret's eyes glittered. "She said she's thinking of having a pianist play on Friday and Saturday nights."

"Wow," Diane said. "That might be a nice addition to Marble Cove's limited entertainment."

"It certainly would," Margaret agreed.

"Well, I'm sorry you had so much trouble at home, but I'm glad you two went out and got to dance, and then brought me dessert!"

"You're right," Margaret said. "This way is better. But I still think I need to learn the art of preparing a meal so that nothing is ruined and everything is ready at once. It will be a big challenge."

"If you really want to do it, I'm sure you can," Allan said.

★ ★ ★

The next morning, Diane slept fairly late but awoke feeling rested. She put on jeans and a sweater and went out to the kitchen. Rocky got up from his bed and stretched. By the time she had the teakettle on, he was waiting by the door.

"All right," Diane said. She let him out into the yard for a couple of minutes, but watched him closely. When he came back to the door, she took him in and fed him. Her tea water was hot, and she pulled a loaf of whole-grain bread from the cupboard.

On one of her trips between the counter and the table, she glanced out the front window and saw Beverly walking slowly down the sidewalk. Something odd about her gait made Diane stop and stare. What was that in her hand? It looked like a strap. The fence that kept Rocky confined blocked her view.

Diane stepped out onto the porch and shut the door behind her. "Hey, Beverly. What are you up to?"

Beverly turned toward her, a look of chagrin on her face. "Oh, hi, Diane. I'm walking my newest family member, if you can believe it."

"What? Let me see!" She hurried down the walk, and Beverly stopped to unlatch the gate in her fence.

"Oh! You're right! I don't believe it." Diane went to her knees and ruffled the playful puppy's fur. He jumped up to put his front paws on her leg and licked her face. "You doll," Diane said. "You absolute living doll!"

She stood and looked at Beverly's face. Beverly was not laughing.

"Tell me everything," Diane insisted. "When did you get him?"

"Yesterday," Beverly said glumly. "He's Jeff's Valentine's Day present to me."

Diane took in her expression and tone. "Oh boy. Can you come in?"

At her friend's hesitation, she quickly shifted gears. "Or let me bring Rocky out. We could walk with you to the end of the street and back to your house."

"All right, if you think they'll get along."

"I'm sure they will. Hold on. I'll get my coat and put him on the leash." Diane dashed back into the house, moving faster than she had in weeks. She pulled on her jacket and gloves. "Come on, boy," she said, slapping her thigh. Rocky barked and leaped to her. Diane clipped on his leash and led him outside. Beverly had moved only a couple of yards beyond the gate with her little gray ball of fluff.

Diane's golden retriever mix looked huge next to the little schnoodle. She kept the leash tight and held Rocky back a few paces, though he whined and leaned eagerly toward the puppy.

"Easy, boy. Be polite." She smiled at Beverly. "What's his name?"

Beverly huffed out a breath. "I don't know."

"You haven't picked anything out yet?" Diane asked.

She shook her head. "I guess I'm in the resistance mode. Subconsciously, I'm probably thinking that if I don't name him, he'll go away."

"Aw!" Diane stepped closer, letting Rocky get within a foot of the pup.

The puppy barked and pulled at his leash, trying to get closer to Rocky. Beverly tensed.

"Take it easy, now," Diane said with a laugh. "Rocky, you be nice." She inched forward until the two dogs touched noses. Soon they were sniffing each other and prancing about their owners.

"Okay, let's see if they'll walk without being too distracted now." Diane set off toward the end of the street, and Beverly brought her puppy along. They all adjusted their strides to the schnoodle's pace. Now and then one of the dogs stopped and tried to socialize with the other.

"Do you think they're getting along all right?" Beverly asked.

"I think they're very excited and they want to play together," Diane said. "I predict that within a few weeks we'll be turning them loose in our yards together while we chat."

"Really? How do we know they won't fight?"

"They've already decided they like each other." Diane smiled brightly at her. "You seem like you're not crazy about being a dog owner, but trust me, he'll grow on you. And he'll be a good companion for your dad too."

"Yes, I thought of that." Beverly sighed. "I've never liked dogs. It irks me that Jeff didn't ask me first, instead of just plunking this creature down on me."

"Did you tell him how you feel about it?"

"No. He was so happy, I couldn't disappoint him."

Diane smiled. "That's part of love."

"Maybe," Beverly said, "but so is communication and knowing your partner well enough not to spring something on her that makes her uncomfortable."

They had reached the parking area at the end of Newport Avenue. The puppy at last paused to "do his duty."

"There," Diane said. "Shall we head back?"

As they strolled past her driveway and on past the Hoskins' house, Diane asked if Beverly had everything she needed for the puppy.

"No. Jeff brought him in a crate, and he did think to bring a bag of puppy food and the leash. That's it."

"Where did the puppy sleep last night?"

"In the crate. That seemed a bit cruel to me, but he didn't seem to mind, and at least I didn't have to worry about him being all over the house during the night."

Diane nodded. "Lots of dogs are 'crate trained.' Their crate is their secure place. But you can get him a doggie bed, if you prefer. And he'll need some toys to chew on. How old is he?"

"I think Jeff said twelve weeks."

"Yeah, he'll be teething some more. And he might outgrow the crate, but I don't think these dogs get real big."

"That's a relief," Beverly said.

"Well, Lee Waters can help you at the Pet Place."

They had reached the Littles' house, and Fred Little was heading out to his car. He waved. "Good morning, ladies."

Diane and Beverly waved and called greetings, walking on toward Beverly's driveway.

"I've been thinking about the train station," Beverly said. "I should be able to find time soon to go look through the Courier's archives again."

"I wish I could do that too," Diane said, "but I don't think I'm up to it yet. All those stairs, and the dust!"

"Don't even think about it yet. I remember when we went together. It was so disorganized. It's a little discouraging even to think about it."

"You might want to try the historical society first," Diane suggested.

"Great idea! Less musty, and I have a feeling they're more user-friendly too. I think I'll go there and look for information on Elias Thorpe and the train station."

"Don't forget the quarry scandal," Diane said.

Beverly nodded. "It may be a few days before I get there, but I do want to go."

They had reached Beverly's house, and Diane stopped walking. "Well, Rocky and I had better say good-bye. It was great talking to you."

"You too." Beverly looked ruefully down at the puppy. "Thanks for all your advice, Diane. I'll make this work for Jeff's sake. I think he's wanted a puppy for at least thirty years."

"And now he has one."

"Ha! Now *I* have one. But yes, if I think of it as an act of love for Jeff, I may be able to overcome at least a small part of my aversion to dogs. At least it's a smallish dog."

Diane patted the sleeve of Beverly's wool coat. "You'll get to like him. I know you will. You're too kindhearted not to."

"I hope you're right." Beverly guided the puppy into the driveway and turned back to wave.

CHAPTER NINE

The four friends met Friday afternoon at Margaret's gallery. Shelley was glad they could all get together—she'd been feeling a little out of the loop with all her baking, family, and business concerns occupying her time. After a brief account of everyone's Valentine's Day adventures, the talk turned eagerly to Beverly's puppy.

"I want to see him," Shelley cried. "I can't believe you've been walking him, and the kids and I haven't spotted him yet."

"Rocky and I just love him," Diane said. "Prize will too—not to mention the kids."

"We'll have so much fun with them this summer," Shelley told Beverly.

Margaret smiled as she poured out four cups of coffee. "It makes me almost feel I should go out and get a dog."

"Oh no," Beverly said. "You do fine with Adelaide's cats. Don't get a dog for the wrong reason."

"That's right," Diane said. "Any time you get a longing, we'll share Rocky and Prize and…Beverly, have you come up with a name yet?"

Beverly ducked her head. "Afraid not. Still in denial."

"You'll find the right one," Shelley said. "Sometimes it takes time."

"Once you get a handle on his personality, it will come to you," Diane said with a smile.

"Diane, how are you doing?" Margaret asked.

"Oh, I'm all right," Diane said.

"Seems like you've been a little down lately," Shelley ventured.

"I suppose I have been, but I appreciate you all so much." Diane laughed. "I couldn't believe it when Allan called me last night, and then he and Margaret brought me cheesecake. It was great. I don't often entertain in my pajamas."

Margaret smiled broadly. "We had such a nice visit."

"Well, I hope you're feeling a hundred percent better soon," Shelley said.

"I think I will," Diane replied. "I know being sick has put a damper on things for me, and I admit the holiday was a little stressful. I've concluded that I'm not ready to have a man in my life all the time."

"Is that about Eric?" Shelley asked.

"Partly, I think, but not completely. I don't really know for sure. But dating seems to have become a bigger issue for me than it should be, so I'm just putting it on hold for a while."

"I hope we didn't add to your stress," Margaret said.

"Same here," Beverly added.

"Yeah," Shelley said, "we didn't mean to push Leo on you."

"You didn't. You all have been wonderful. I suspect you just want me to be in a happy relationship, the way you all are." Diane smiled at Margaret. "How did Adelaide's evening go with her friends?"

"Pretty well, I'd say. The housemother took them out to eat, and then they went to a movie."

The doorbell jangled as two customers entered.

"Excuse me, ladies," Margaret said. "Help yourselves to more coffee and cookies."

"I'll make another pot," Shelley said as Margaret went off to wait on the customers. "We about emptied that one." As she went about freshening the coffee, Diane and Beverly carried everyone's half-full mugs out to Margaret's office.

When Shelley joined them, Diane said, "I'm dying to know what you decide about the Cove, Shelley. When is it you start filling in for Rusty?"

"Monday." Shelley told Beverly about her agreement with Rusty for the duration of his vacation, and his offer to pass the reins of the business to her in late spring.

"Wow, that would be a huge adjustment for you," Beverly said.

"You're telling me. But next week will be a good practice run." Shelley sipped her coffee.

"We'll all come in and visit you next week," Diane promised.

"What will you do about the kids?" Beverly asked.

"That's what everybody's asking, including me. Dan's trying to get more time off, and Frances had said she'll help some of the time. Margaret's agreed to let Adelaide go to my house on two days when she doesn't have afternoon classes. I may have to run and pick the kids up from school, but Brenna will cover at the Cove. Adelaide can stay with the children for a short time. I think with everybody helping, we'll get through it."

"If I can pop over to help, let me know," Diane said.

"Thanks. Arranging child care for one week is telling me how hard it would be to do it full-time." Shelley looked at her watch. "Well, I hate to leave while Margaret's still busy, but I'd better get home. Adelaide is wonderful with the kids, but I don't like to leave them too long. I'll see you all later."

She zipped her parka and pulled on her gloves. Diane and Beverly called farewells, and she went out into the gallery. Margaret stood behind the counter, bending over some papers. More people had come into the gallery, and Shelley was glad she hadn't decided to wait until Margaret was free.

"I'm heading out," Shelley told her softly. "Nice to talk to you, if only for a few minutes."

"Thanks for coming, Shelley! See you again soon," Margaret said.

★ ★ ★

The next morning, Shelley got out the door early for her delivery run. It was Dan's day off, Saturday, and she hoped to have time to talk to Rusty some more about her duties before customers began to arrive. When she got to the Cove, the owner had unlocked the back door and begun setting up for the morning rush. Shelley carried in two boxes of muffins and pastries.

"Oh, great, you're here," Rusty said. "I asked Brenna to set up a schedule when she and the other people can work during the week you'll be here. She left it right over here," He took a sheet of paper in a plastic protector from the counter.

"Great," Shelley said, skimming down it. "And it looks like Brenna's planning to close up shop some evenings."

"Right. You won't have to stay late on those nights. I know you won't want to every day, with your family and all."

"Thanks, Rusty. This looks workable."

He showed her a few more things like how to open the cash register in the morning and stock it with change for the early rush of coffee-drinkers. They went over the process of taking credit cards.

"Brenna will be here with you the first two mornings," Rusty said. "She's the most knowledgeable of my workers. And one other person will be here for the morning rush with you every day."

"And they all know how to take plastic, right?" Shelley asked. She was still a little nervous about the procedure, though she had begun to take credit cards in her bakery business. The machine was different here, and so was the confirmation process.

"Everybody's had the training, but some are more proficient than others."

"Gotcha." Shelley decided right then to pay close attention those first couple of mornings, when Brenna would be within speaking distance.

"I'll tell ya, this is a big relief to me, knowing you'll be here," Rusty said. "Most of the employees are kids. There's got to be someone over twenty-one here to handle things if anything happens, ya know?"

Shelley gulped. She wasn't used to being the oldest, most reliable member of a team. "Sure, Rusty. Nothing's going to happen. We'll have a wonderful time, and you and Wendy will too."

She hoped it was true, and that things really would go smoothly while he was away.

* * *

Diane typed rapidly. A new clue had come to her, either in her sleep or as she sleepily went about her morning routine, and suddenly she couldn't get it down fast enough. Exhilaration surged through her as the words appeared on the computer screen. Maybe this book would be better than her first two, after all. This clue would set her sleuth off on a new trail leading to a discovery that would—

The screen went black.

Diane froze, her hands above the keyboard.

"No," she said out loud. She waited a few seconds, but nothing changed. The screen stared back at her, black and empty.

"Don't panic," she told herself. She sent up a quick prayer for wisdom. When she opened her eyes, Rocky was standing beside her chair, gazing up at her with huge brown eyes. She patted his head. "It'll be okay, boy."

Immediately she set about doing all the things she knew how to do, rebooting the computer and checking her modem. Still nothing changed.

She sat back in defeat. Burning tears filled her eyes. She felt like screaming, but that would take too much energy.

A knock on the door saved her from wallowing deeper in her despair. She shoved the chair back. Rocky yelped and jumped out of her way.

"Sorry," she said. She took a quick look at his feet, but she didn't think she'd run over his toes; she had only scared him. She hurried out to the front door.

Leo Spangler stood on the doorstep with a paper deli bag in one hand and a cardboard drink tray with two cups in the other.

"Leo!"

"Hi." He eyed her cautiously. "I was doing my Saturday shopping, and I took a chance that you hadn't eaten yet. I picked up a couple of sandwiches." He arched his eyebrows and waited, hopeful and vulnerable.

"That's so nice of you. Come on in."

They went to the kitchen, and Leo set the items down and opened the bag.

"I got a turkey club and a ham and cheese."

"You pick," she said.

"No, really. What sounds best to you?"

She smiled. "Why don't we share—half and half?"

"Great idea."

She took down two plates and a knife. While Leo cut the sandwiches, she got out napkins. "What are the drinks?"

"Smoothies."

"Yum."

Leo grinned. "Looks like I guessed right. Strawberry or pineapple?"

"Strawberry." Diane knew he liked pineapple, and it wasn't her favorite. She sat down opposite him.

They ate for a couple minutes with their comments centering on the sandwiches, which were delicious.

"You know, this was the perfect interruption for me," Diane said. "I probably wouldn't have even stopped for lunch, except that my computer crashed right before you came. Anyway, thanks. I'm glad I didn't have to fix something for myself."

"What's wrong with the computer?" Leo asked.

"I don't know. It just went black all of a sudden while I was working."

"Ouch. I hope you didn't lose much."

She grimaced. "Me too. I try to remember to save frequently, but when I'm typing along and it's flowing well, sometimes I forget."

Rocky came to the table and stood watching them eat, his tail flicking slowly back and forth. Diane looked at him. He wasn't exactly begging, but he stared at every morsel she lifted to her mouth.

"You big baby. It's not like I didn't feed you." She got up, took a dog treat from a canister on the counter, and tossed it to him. Rocky caught it and padded to his bed.

Leo laughed. "They can almost talk, can't they?"

"Sometimes I think he can. How's Limo?"

"He's good." Leo sipped his drink. "Why don't you let me take a look at your computer when we're done? I might see something you missed."

"That would be great. I hate to take it in for service when I don't know what's wrong."

When they had finished the sandwiches, she said, "I think I have a few cookies Shelley brought me in the cupboard."

"I don't usually eat dessert," Leo said, "but that sounds good. That Shelley is a terrific baker."

"Oh, I know! Coffee?"

"Sure."

"I should have started it earlier. It will just take a few minutes." She rose and took their dishes to the counter.

"Mind if I look at the computer while you do that?" Leo asked.

"Go right ahead." She waved him toward her study.

Diane took her time arranging their mugs on a tray and pouring a small ceramic pitcher with cream. She recalled that Leo didn't sweeten his coffee, so she didn't add the sugar bowl. She put half a dozen of Shelley's macadamia-white chip cookies on a small plate. When the coffeemaker had finished dripping, she filled the mugs. Everything was ready, and she had no excuse to linger in the kitchen, so she carried the tray into her study.

"Oh, wow!"

Leo was sitting in her desk chair, eyeing the now bright screen and tapping a few keys.

"Hey, I think it's all set." He swiveled around to face her, grinning.

"What did you do?" she asked.

"Not a lot. You had left it shut down, and when I turned it on again an error message came up. I basically followed it through the prompts to get rid of a threat."

"A threat?" She set the tray on the file cabinet.

Leo shrugged. "It said there was a threat and it needed to quarantine the program. I do think it's taken care of now. You have a good security system."

"Thanks." Diane still wasn't sure, but the on-screen desktop looked normal now. She held out a mug to him.

"Oh, thanks." Leo stood. "Why don't you check it out and see if you lost the file you were working on?"

To Diane's delight, her manuscript was intact, except for the last two paragraphs she had written. She could restore those in minutes.

"I don't know how to thank you," she said. "I have very little patience for computers."

"You probably would have figured it out," he said, reaching for a cookie. He sat down on a straight chair she kept near the desk for visitors.

Diane picked up her mug and selected a cookie. She had the vague feeling that she ought to talk to him about their relationship, but the idea of getting into a big discussion about feelings and nuances seemed a bit daunting just now. Couldn't they take it from here—this successful moment of camaraderie—and see where things led naturally?

"So…how are things going at the clinic?" she asked.

"Good. We've got a dog spending the weekend posttrauma, and I went over to feed him and check on him this morning. I'll go back before dinner tonight."

"Is he badly injured?"

Leo shook his head. "He'll be okay."

The doorbell rang, and Diane lifted her chin. "I wonder who that is. Would you excuse me?"

"Sure," Leo said.

It was probably Shelley or Beverly, come to check on her, Diane thought as she went to the door.

She pulled the door open and stood still, staring. Martin Stilwell stood on her front porch, his dark hair tousled. He wore an open ski parka with a forest-green sweater under it, and brown corduroy pants.

"Hello, Mrs. Spencer." His anxious expression and tentative tone made her heart lurch. She looked past him toward his car, but apparently he was alone.

"Martin! Where's Jessica?"

"She's in Boston. I came by myself. I hope you don't mind."

Diane didn't know what to think, but she wanted to find out pronto what was going on. "Come on in. I've got coffee. Would you like some?"

Leo was standing in the kitchen doorway.

"Martin, you've met my friend, Leo Spangler."

"Hi, Martin." Leo stepped forward and set his coffee mug on the table. "Diane, I should get going. It was nice talking to you."

"Yes, thanks for stopping by, and thanks for lunch." She snagged Leo's jacket from the back of the chair he'd sat in earlier and handed it to him.

"Nice to see you, Dr. Spangler," Martin said.

Leo nodded. "Same here."

Diane walked with him to the door.

"Can I call you later?" Leo asked quietly as he stepped out.

"Sure. And thanks for everything—the computer—well, you know."

She shut the door and turned back to the kitchen. Martin had a lot of explaining to do.

CHAPTER TEN

I'm sorry to bother you," Martin said.

"You're not bothering me." Diane poured coffee for him and set the sugar bowl over near him. Now where was the creamer? Oh yes, she'd left it in the study, where she and Leo had enjoyed their coffee. "Do you take cream?"

"No, thanks."

She sat down. "What's happened, Martin?"

"Nothing." His soft brown eyes took on a bit of panic. "Not really."

"You didn't drive all the way up here for no reason," Diane said.

He sighed and ran a hand through his hair. "I wondered if I could talk to you, since my...my problem has to do with Jessica."

"Of course." She stuffed down the automatic defensiveness that sprang up when he mentioned a problem in the same sentence with her daughter's name. If she wanted to help, she needed to remain objective.

"I just feel like I need a little advice from someone—you know—older and wiser? I mean, my mom's gone, and my father and I aren't close. So if you—"

"Martin." His fidgeting and meandering didn't relieve Diane's apprehension. Still, she was glad he felt safe in coming to her. She reached over and clasped his hand. "Whatever it is, just spit it out."

His eyes widened. "Sure."

For a fleeting moment, Diane thought, *He's going to break off the engagement! Poor Jessica!*

Martin gulped. "I guess it's career advice I need. That and…and how to put it to Jessica."

"Career advice?" Diane almost laughed, but managed to keep a grip on herself, despite the relief flooding through her. "Are you not happy with your job?"

"Well, uh…" He picked up his mug and took a sip of the coffee, set the mug down, and straightened his shoulders. "You know I'm in IT."

"Yes, information technology, right?"

He nodded. "It's a good job, and I make a good salary, but…"

Comprehension dawned. "But your heart isn't in it."

"Is it that obvious?"

"Now it is." Diane wished she was his own mom and could give him a hug. She'd have to use a different approach for this young man. "Do you just not like what you do every day?"

He shifted in his chair. "It's okay, but I guess you could say the novelty has worn off. I'm always doing something slightly different, and yet it's the same, you know? Day after day, the same thing, stuck in front of a computer screen."

"I can imagine." Diane smiled at him. "How long have you felt this way?"

"For the last year or two. When I met Jessica, everything was different. Better, I mean." Even his eyes brightened when he talked about her.

Diane smiled. "So you kept on with what you were doing?"

"Yeah. I didn't want to move away when I'd just met the most fantastic girl, and—well, the pay *is* good. Did I say that?"

"Yes, and I do understand. I used to live in the city too. It takes a good salary to live in Boston and have the freedom to do the things you want to do."

He nodded.

"What is it you think you would like to change to?" Diane asked gently.

"Well, I've always loved history. I majored in that in my undergrad years."

She thought at once of Beverly's father. "Do you want to teach?"

He shrugged. "Yes, I think so. But I'd have to go back to school to qualify."

"How much schooling would you need? Don't you have a master's already?"

"Yes, in technology. It's the education courses I'd need." He sipped his coffee and looked at her over the rim of his cup.

"Have you looked into this?" Diane asked.

"Yeah. I could qualify in a year for a teaching certificate, if I packed the courses in. But I can't do that and keep working full-time at what I do. If I keep the job I've got, I figure it will take me two years, plus a semester of student teaching."

"But you could do it all in a year if that was all you did?"

He nodded. "But I wouldn't have any income during that time, and after I finished the course work—well, teaching doesn't pay nearly as much as IT."

"So, either way, you're talking about a severe drop in salary."

"Right. And I might have to move when I finished, depending on where my next job was."

Diane frowned as she thought over his options. "And why is it that you haven't talked to Jessica about all this?"

Martin puffed out a breath. "I guess I'm afraid she won't like it. Her plans all seem to depend on staying in the city. She's been looking into housing options. Last week she asked me if I'd consider reserving a condominium in a swanky new development. The condos are gorgeous, but…well, the price." He looked up at her. "Oh, we could afford it, but that's assuming Jessica and I both keep the jobs we have now. But even if we did—I mean, do we really want to spend that much of our income on housing? Personally, I don't need an aristocratic address."

"And you think Jessica does?"

"I don't know. Her apartment now isn't pretentious. But those condos…" Martin shook his head. "I just don't see us living there."

"Then you need to say so." Diane sat back and studied his troubled face. "Martin, maybe Jessica doesn't want that either. But since you haven't told her what you *do* want, maybe she thinks you'd like the new condos."

Rocky came over to Diane's side and whined.

"How about going for a walk with Rocky and me?" Diane asked Martin.

"Sure. That'd be good."

"Terrific. You get his leash—it's right over there by the door—and I'll rig up." She put on her outdoor gear, and they headed down to the beach. The wind was cool, but not too bad.

"It's really beautiful here," Martin said. "You have a great location."

"Thanks." Diane let Rocky off the leash so he could run up and down the empty beach for a few minutes. She turned to Martin. "Know what I think?"

His eyes widened in question.

"You and Jessica need a frank, open discussion," Diane said. "It's not fair to her not to let her know what's on your mind. She's trying to plan a wedding, but more than that, you need to start out your marriage with good communication."

"I know you're right."

"Take her someplace private," Diane suggested, beginning to stroll down the beach in the direction Rocky had taken. Martin kept pace with her. "Maybe you could cook dinner for her at your place. Nothing elaborate, though, or that would be too distracting. Hey, pick up a pizza."

He laughed for the first time. "Now you're talking. I'm not much of a cook."

"Well, I know Jessica loves you, and she wants you to be happy. I can't speak for my daughter, but I'm inclined to think that she would agree to a change like you're describing, and that she'd support you all the way. However, I also know that she loves her job. She might not be ready to leave the law firm. Do you think you could commute to a teaching job in the suburbs?"

"Maybe. Well, sure. I'm willing to make sacrifices if she's open to giving it a try."

"Okay, so that's one thing you're committed to."

He nodded.

"And for the first year at least, it wouldn't be much of a problem, would it? Where would you take your classes?"

"Probably at BU. That's about a half hour for me from my place, but if we kept Jessica's apartment, it would be closer by bus."

"There you go," Diane said. "That's a starting place, but look at other options. If she doesn't want to keep her apartment, consider both your commutes from your place or a new location. This will take some research, Martin."

"I'm good at that." Martin smiled at her. "Thanks a lot."

"I'm not sure I've helped much," Diane said.

"Yes, you have. You've made me realize how important it is to discuss this with Jessica. And you know, I might be able to keep on with my company part-time while I went to school. Or if not that, I could do some IT work as a freelancer. I've made a lot of contacts over the last few years. I'm sure I could get some independent contracts."

"That might be good—you could set your own hours. Why don't you look into those options and get some concrete numbers before you make a final decision? But, Martin, Jessica should be in on this with you. Don't put off telling her any longer."

"I won't."

"She may have ideas you haven't thought of yet," Diane added.

"Yeah, she might. She knows a lot of people too, and she's really smart. I guess the money thing is the worst part, from my way of thinking."

"What? You don't like the idea of Jessica earning more than you do, or what?"

Martin kicked at a clump of seaweed. "It's not that so much as...well, lately she seems to have all these ideas for the wedding that seem kind of..."

"Over the top?" Diane asked tentatively. Would Jessica really want a money-is-no-object blowout, or was she just trying out ideas for a fantasy wedding? She'd always been a fairly practical girl.

"I'd hate to spend half a year's income on that one day," Martin said mournfully.

Diane eyed him closely. "Do you really think she'd do that?"

"Maybe. She mentioned renting out a museum for the reception. It's like ten thousand dollars just for that."

Diane drew in a deep breath. She vaguely recalled Jessica rattling on about a fabulous wedding she had attended the previous summer. "Jessica might be influenced by some of the women she works with. Or maybe she's just throwing out wild ideas to get your reaction. On the other hand, maybe that's what she really wants." Diane didn't think that was the case, but she tried to be fair. She also tried to keep from leaping to Jessica's defense when she didn't know the whole story. "Martin, have you ever given her any reason to think you might not go on earning as much as you are now? Or that you think some of her spending ideas are excessive?"

"Probably not. I've been sort of sidestepping the issue, I admit. I was afraid we'd fight about it. But that's not realistic, I guess. Jessica doesn't get angry easily."

"Well, you should ask her if this is really what she wants."

"So…you think she could be happy with the lifestyle I could give her? As a teacher, I mean?"

Diane smiled. "You'll have to ask her that question. And quit stewing about it and being afraid of her reaction. Get it out there." She glanced at her watch. "We should go back." She whistled to Rocky, and he came bounding over the cold sand. She handed Martin the leash. When Rocky got to them, she stooped and patted him. "Good boy."

Martin clipped the leash to the dog's collar and they headed back toward the boardwalk. The sun was already moving down the sky behind the town.

"Look, time is getting on," Diane said. "Would you like to have supper here and spend the night on my couch?"

Martin looked startled and pushed his sleeve up so he could glance at his watch. "That's not necessary, but thank you. I really should get back to Boston tonight. I'm sorry—I shouldn't have taken up so much of your time."

"Not a problem," Diane said. "If you're tired, you should wait."

"I'll be all right. And if I leave right away, I might get home in time to talk to Jessica tonight."

A few minutes later Rocky was back in the house. Diane stood in the driveway with Martin, next to his car.

"Thanks awfully for your help," he said.

Diane drew him close and stood on tiptoe to kiss his cheek. "Thanks for coming all this way to see me. I know you're serious about your relationship with Jessica."

"I love her so much." Martin blinked twice, but she saw the sheen in his eyes. "We'll work it out."

She nodded. "Drive safe. I'll be praying for you two."

CHAPTER ELEVEN

Beverly took the puppy inside after a short turn about the yard. Her father had offered to take him out, but the last thing she wanted was her father slipping on the ice. She foresaw many frigid walks for her and the little gray pest between now and spring.

When they went inside, her father was in the kitchen, pouring himself a cup of decaffeinated coffee. He smiled at the puppy.

"Hey there, Junior! Is it cold outside?"

"Don't call him that," Beverly snapped.

"He's part of the family now," her father said, bending down to pat the pup's head.

"Even if he is, his name's not *Junior*." Beverly shuddered.

"Okay, what *is* his name?" her father asked. "If you don't like what I call him, you'd better come up with something you like."

Beverly sighed and unbuttoned her coat. She didn't want to get into an argument over the dog. The whole situation made her feel as though a huge wave had plowed over her.

"I just don't know if I can keep him, Father."

"What are you talking about?" He peered at her sternly over his glasses. "If you feel that strongly about it, you should have told Jeff on Thursday. It's kind of late now. You don't seriously want him to get rid of the puppy, do you?"

"I don't know," Beverly wailed. She put her hands to her temples. "You know I don't like dogs. I've never been comfortable around them. And Mrs. Peabody doesn't like him either. She was complaining about it just this noon. She said we can't expect her to help out with him and that she didn't sign up for dodging animals in the kitchen or letting them in and out all day."

"Aw, don't worry about Mrs. Peabody. She'll get over it."

Beverly glared at him. "What if she doesn't? And what if I don't?"

Her father held up both hands. "Now, don't shoot the messenger."

"Please, Father," Beverly said. "I'm trying my best here. And no, I don't think I can ask Jeff to get rid of the puppy now. That's the whole problem, don't you see? I don't want to disappoint Jeff." The puppy was frisking about the kitchen, stopping periodically to look up at her and whine. She sighed. "Guess I'd better feed the little mutt."

"Oh, that reminds me," her father said. "We're getting a little low on the puppy food. That bag Jeff brought is nearly gone."

"And tomorrow's Sunday. I guess I'd better go to the pet store now." Beverly started to button up again. "Do you want to go along?"

"Sure," her father said. "We can take Junior with us."

Beverly scowled. "Oh no. I'm not going into a store with him. I just want to get what I need and get home. And *stop* calling him that!"

Her father's face drooped. "All right. I'll stay home with him. But get a big bag!"

Beverly dashed upstairs to get her purse. When she came down, all was quiet. She looked into the living room. Her father had settled in his recliner and had the news on. Beside him on the end table was his coffee mug, and the gray puppy lay in her father's lap, with his chin on his paws.

Beverly let out a sigh. "I'll see you two later."

"Bye," her father called.

She stepped out onto the driveway. Twilight was falling. Out on the sidewalk, someone walked slowly along, and when he came even with the end of the drive, she realized it was Dan Bauer, with Prize on a leash.

"Hi, Dan." She waved.

"Hello, Beverly." Dan stopped and called, "I hear you've got a new dog."

"More like a dog-ette. He's just a puppy, and even when he's grown I don't think he'll be any bigger than Prize."

Dan laughed and looked down at Aiden's dog, a beagle-cocker spaniel mix. "Sounds like they might make good playmates."

"You may be right." Beverly gestured toward her car. "I'm going to the pet store now for more dog food. Do you need anything?"

"I don't think so, but thanks. Guess we'd better get home. Shelley and I are going out tonight."

"Oh, is this your late Valentine's dinner?" Beverly asked.

"Yeah. You know about that?"

She smiled. "Yes, and I think it's sweet. Have fun."

"Thanks." Dan turned back toward home, and Beverly got into the car and started the engine.

"You may as well stop complaining and join the canine lovers of the community," she told herself out loud. "That puppy is not going away."

* * *

Diane heard nothing from Jessica or Martin Saturday evening or Sunday morning. She began to wonder how things had gone, or if they'd even managed to get together to talk. At four o'clock, she decided she'd better take Rocky out one last time for the day, before it got dark. Before she could get up out of her chair, the phone rang.

"Mom! Hi!"

"Jessica," Diane said cautiously, "I'm so glad you called."

"I'll bet." Jessica laughed. "Martin told me how he surprised you yesterday."

"We had a good visit. It was very nice to see him."

"Oh, Mom, I'm sorry he put you on the spot, but thanks so much for being there for him and—well, for being *you*."

Diane exhaled. "I take it this means you've hashed things over?"

"We've started anyway. I had no idea. Can you imagine him being so unhappy in his job and never dropping me a hint?"

"I'm glad it's out in the open now. He obviously cares a lot about keeping you happy."

"He sure does. To the point where he'd probably have an ulcer if he didn't open up pretty soon."

"So…tell me what happened." Diane settled back in her chair.

"We went to church this morning. I was out last night. My friend Lindsay and I went to the movies. When I got home, I saw that Martin had called, but it was kind of late, so I put it off until this morning. He never said anything until after church, Mom. Can you believe it?"

"Yeah, I can. He's been guarding his secret pretty carefully."

"I felt so bad. I was shocked when he told me he'd driven all the way to your house. But when he started talking about his work, I realized he had given me little clues before. He said once that he might not want to stay with the company forever. I just thought he meant he might move on to another IT job. It never occurred to me that he wanted to get into a new field."

"He probably hoped you'd pick up on it and dig into the subject," Diane said. "It must have been hard for him to lay it all out there for you."

"I think practicing on you first was a big help." Jessica sounded quite happy now. "Mom, he had some ideas on what he might do. I heard him out, and I told him that, of course, I wanted him to be able to change careers if that's what he wants. And I think he'll make a fantastic teacher!"

"So do I," Diane said.

"Well, I felt awful when I realized how pressured I'd made him feel. Mom, I had no idea. I mean, a big wedding isn't that important to me."

"I'm glad to hear it. And honey, I'd like to chip in on the wedding costs. I hope you know that."

"Thanks. I think we can have a very nice wedding that won't wipe out our savings or upset Martin. I just had no clue what he really wanted because he wouldn't talk about it. I came up with several suggestions, but he'd just back away and not comment. Now I can see how stressful that was for him."

"I'm sure he's feeling a lot better now," Diane said.

"I hope so. And—did he mention to you about where we're going to live?"

"He, uh, said some things about your place and his, but he also mentioned some new condos."

"Well, we're going to forget about the condos," Jessica said firmly. "I told him I'm willing to keep on living in either my apartment or his—though they're both pretty small— while he takes the courses he needs."

"That's very generous of you, and I think it's wise."

"And when he gets a teaching job," Jessica went on, "we can decide where we want to live more permanently. Who knows what will happen by then? I may be ready to move to a new job too."

"I'm glad you're so supportive of him," Diane said.

"Oh, Mom, I feel like such an idiot! We still have a lot of things to work out, but he seemed relieved. And you know what? I think we'll have a lot of fun planning all of this. Almost as much fun as I'll have planning the wedding, now that I know what the budget is."

"You have a wedding budget?"

"I do now," Jessica said with a laugh. "We talked about what we both thought was reasonable, and we settled on a figure in between."

"Well, you can either add my contribution to that, or use it to help you put some of your own money and Martin's into savings," Diane said.

"Thanks, Mom. You're sweet. I'll see what Martin thinks about that. I'm done making decisions without talking to him."

* * *

On Monday morning, Shelley got out of the house early for her first day at the Cove, before the children were awake. Dan was meeting Wayne, his boss, an hour later than usual, so that he'd be able to take Aiden and Hailey to school. He had also promised to drop Emma at his mother's before going to work.

Frances would collect Aiden and Hailey, and the plan was for her to leave them and Emma with Adelaide at the Hoskins' house. Allan would supervise Adelaide's stint of caregiving without interfering unless necessary. Shelley was glad he'd be nearby. And she didn't even want to think about the arrangements she had cobbled together for the rest of the week.

Was this really worth it? She unlocked the back door of the store and carried in her boxes of pastries. Brenna had offered to meet her there, but Shelley had assured her that she could handle it, and she didn't want Brenna to have to come in early and stay late on the same day. The schedule showed that a college student would arrive at opening time to help her with the morning rush.

She started a pot of regular coffee first and went down Rusty's list of morning preparations. Unlock the cash register and stock it with change; check all the tables for cleanliness; stock the counter area where customers doctored their coffee; turn on the espresso machine.

The time flew, and she was surprised when a knock came at the back door. She opened it cautiously. A thin young man with dark, curly hair stood outside.

"Are you Parker?" she asked.

"Yes, ma'am. I'll be here until ten."

"Great. Come on in." She swung the door wide. "I'm Shelley. I'm taking Rusty's place this week."

"He told me. What do you want me to do?"

"We've got fifteen minutes," Shelley said. "Do you know how to run the espresso machine? I thought I did everything exactly the way Rusty showed me, but it doesn't seem to be heating the milk or the coffee."

"*Hmm*, I'm not much good with machinery," Parker said as he took off his jacket. He went to the machine and tried making a cup of espresso, but what came out was cloudy cold water. "That's not right."

"Ick," Shelley said. She checked everything she could think of, but found no solution. "What'll we do?"

A sound at the front door drew her attention. Glancing at the clock, she realized it was time to open. She waved to the customer—she recognized one of the clerks from the Mercantile—and hurried to unlock the door for him.

"Good morning!"

"Am I early?" he asked.

"No, I just didn't realize what time it was. I'm Shelley, and I'm filling in for Rusty this week."

"Shelley—you're the one who makes the muffins and stuff?"

"That's right."

He laughed. "Great. That's the biggest reason I come here."

"What can I get you this morning?"

"Just coffee and one of those blueberry muffins."

Other customers came in, and before long Shelley was fighting with the espresso machine again. Brenna wouldn't be in until Parker's shift ended at ten, but what would she do in the meantime, with all the early regulars who liked their lattes and double espressos on the way to work?

At last she gave up and went back to the counter.

"I'm sorry," she told the waiting customer. "The machine isn't cooperating right now. It may be a little while before we can make lattes."

"I can't wait," the woman said. "Just give me regular coffee instead."

"Sure." Shelley poured her a cup to go and waved away her money. "On the house this morning, and I'm sorry."

The next customer stepped forward. "I'll take a raspberry Danish and a vanilla latte."

Shelley gulped. "I'm sorry. I can't do the latte right now. But I'll give you a cup of coffee for free and only charge you for the Danish."

She was going to lose a pile of money this morning, but she didn't know what else to do.

The next customer wanted espresso. She explained the situation and then hurried over to Parker. "Look, for anyone who asks for a drink that you need to make on that machine, tell them we'll give them free regular coffee instead. I'll make an extra pot right now, and then I'm calling Brenna."

Parker nodded as he counted out change for his customer.

Shelley moved the half-empty pot of coffee to the warmer and started a new pot, then dashed to the phone. Customers were now three deep at the counter.

"Hello?" Brenna sounded sleepy.

"Hi, it's Shelley. I'm really, really, really sorry to bother you, but the espresso machine isn't working. Help!"

"Oh, that's happened befo-uh," Brenna said, her Downeast accent thick. "You checked to make sure it's plugged in, right?"

"Yes, the lights come on and everything, and all the reservoirs are loaded—it even spits out something, but you wouldn't call it coffee."

"Okay." After what sounded like a yawn, Brenna said. "I'll be there in twenty minutes, but you'd better call the repairman now."

"You don't need to come in early. Parker's here. But are you sure I should go ahead and call the repairman?" Shelley looked over her shoulder at the line of fidgety coffee-lovers.

"Yeah, his number's on the laminated list by the phone. Ex-Perk Repair."

Shelley blinked. "Okay, and if that's the only way to go with this, you probably don't need to come in yet."

"All right, I'll see you late-uh. And Shelley—hang tough."

She laughed. "Thanks." She clicked off the connection and punched in the repairman's number. No one answered, but who would at six thirty in the morning? The voice mail message played, and she said, "Please come to the Cove on Main Street in Marble Cove immediately. Our espresso machine isn't working." She gave the store's phone number twice and hung up.

Parker was besieged by customers, all of whom seemed a bit edgy. *Must be caffeine addicts,* Shelley thought. She stepped up beside Parker and pasted a big smile on her face. She couldn't give away the store while Rusty was gone, but she didn't want to alienate his best customers either.

CHAPTER TWELVE

"S cat! You get out of here!"

Mrs. Peabody's strident voice cautioned Beverly that she had not warmed up to the newest addition to the Wheeland household. She entered the kitchen expecting the older woman to vent her anger, and she was not disappointed.

"You've got to keep that mutt out of here. I refuse to cook in a kitchen with a dog in it." Mrs. Peabody glared at Beverly. "Look what he did!" She held out the brown calico oven mitt she favored. One side had a large, ragged hole in it, and the bias trim around the cuff hung in limp shreds.

Beverly swallowed hard. The puppy had chewed one of her father's slippers last night, and before they'd discovered his misdeed, the slipper was ruined. She could understand why Mrs. Peabody was upset.

"What's going on?" her father boomed from the doorway behind her.

"It's that fool dog," Mrs. Peabody muttered. "He's destructive, that's what he is."

Beverly took the oven mitt and held it out silently for him to inspect. Mrs. Peabody turned back to the work counter and slammed her measuring cups and steel mixing bowl harder than was necessary.

"Oh well, he's just a baby," her father said. "He's teething, and he's got to chew on something."

"Well, he doesn't have to chew on things I use to fix what you eat! Haven't you ever heard of germs?"

Beverly's stomach twisted. "I got him a rubber toy..."

"He needs something that tastes better," her father said. "Maybe some of those rawhide chews."

Great, Beverly thought. *Another trip to the store.* She had planned to spend this morning at the municipal building, but she couldn't leave them like this.

"I'll go to the pet store. Maybe you can put him in his cage while I'm gone."

"No," her father said, his eyebrows lowered. "We don't want to shut him up during the day. I'll take him into the library with me."

"Well, make sure he's got something you don't mind him gnawing on, or he'll be chewing the furniture legs," Mrs. Peabody cautioned.

Her father moved toward the cupboard. "I will. Pardon me while I fix myself a cup of tea."

Mrs. Peabody threw him a glance of displeasure but said nothing.

"I'll go get my purse," Beverly said. Maybe she could get the rawhide chews at the Mercantile, where she could also buy a new oven mitt for Mrs. Peabody. If not, she'd head over to the Pet Place. And one of these days she'd have to get her father a new pair of slippers.

"You'd better take the puppy out one more time before you leave," her father said. "It's been awhile since you had him outside."

Beverly closed her eyes and silently counted to ten.

* * *

"Folks, in case you didn't hear, our machine is down, so no lattes, cappuccino, or espresso right now, but we have plenty of regular and decaf coffee. In fact, we're serving it up on the house for the next"—she glanced down the line—"ten minutes." After this crowd was mollified, they could treat the customers who came in on a case-by-case basis. "Parker, why don't you take the orders and the money, and I'll get their food."

"I wasn't going to get espresso," one man said, "but how about a free muffin instead?"

Before Shelley could speak up, Parker said, "Uh, okay. I guess."

Shelley bit her tongue and handed out free muffins to the man and the two behind him. Soon the crowd thinned. As she'd hoped, within a few minutes, most of the patrons, if not happy, were at least satisfied.

"A regular and a decaf to go," Parker said, "and one cinnamon scone and a bran muffin with those."

"Okay, and you can stop giving away pastries now. Just coffee, okay?" she said quietly.

"Uh, sure. Sorry."

When she had handed over the order and Parker had collected the money for the pastries, they at last had a moment to breathe.

"Did you get the repairman?" Parker asked.

"No. I left a message. We need a better plan, but I'm not sure what to do. If an order involves the espresso machine, then offer customers the regular coffee on the house, but make it clear that it's just this once, until we get the machine fixed. And if they're still upset, then you can offer them a free muffin." If need be, she could whip up an extra batch of muffins in the Cove's kitchen and not charge Rusty for them.

"Got it," Parker said as the door swung open and Augie Jackson ambled in.

Shelley's eyes misted up. A friendly face at last. When Augie reached the counter, she leaned toward him and said, "Good morning, Augie!"

"Hello, Shelley. I came in earlier than my usual time today to see how you're doing."

"You wouldn't believe it," she said.

"Try me."

"The espresso machine's broken and I'm losing money hand over fist, giving away plain coffee to everyone who usually buys a fancy drink."

Augie smiled sympathetically. "Well, I usually drink regular coffee anyway, so you won't lose money on me."

Shelley's lip trembled. "Thanks, Augie, but I'll give you yours too, since you're so sweet."

"Oh no, you don't." Augie reached for his wallet. "I came expecting to pay, and I'm going to pay. And give me one of your divine Danish too."

"Cheese, raspberry, or apple?"

"Mm, that apple sounds good. You don't always have that."

Shelley went around the counter and held out her arms to Augie. "Give me a hug."

"Glad to." Augie squeezed her for a moment and then let her go. "Sweetest breakfast I've had in a long time."

The front door opened and four people came in, making straight for the counter.

"Back to work," Shelley said, and scooted behind the counter to get Augie's coffee and Danish.

After that, things went more smoothly, despite the broken machinery. The tables in the eating area stayed fairly full for two hours. The repairman called at eight and arrived at nine. Brenna came in on his heels, an hour earlier than scheduled. She charmed the customers, especially the regulars, and most of them didn't seem too put out with the substitutions. By the time Parker left for his college classes, the espresso machine was fixed, and it almost seemed like a normal Monday at the Cove.

"We're getting low on pastries already," Brenna observed.

"I gave away a few, to people who seemed upset about their lattes," Shelley confessed, without mentioning Parker's role. "But you know what? I've got a couple dozen Danish and some cookies in my freezer at home. I could run over and get some."

Two men came in, and Shelley thought they looked familiar.

"Still giving free coffee and muffins?" one of them asked.

Shelley smiled, realizing they'd been in shortly after she opened and were among the first to benefit from her largesse. "No, our machine's fixed now."

"Aw, rats," his friend said.

Shelley shook her head. "Nice try, fellas. Hey, I'm about to make a pastry run, but there are two chocolate chip cookies left, and if you want to buy your lattes now, I'll give you the last two cookies."

They anted up, and Shelley slipped out the back door, knowing Brenna wouldn't put up with any nonsense while she was gone. From here on, everyone would pay full price.

When they had time, she and Brenna cleaned up the mess the repairman had left. By five o'clock, traffic in the store had slacked off to an occasional diehard.

Brenna grinned at Shelley. "You may as well head out. I know you've got kids to deal with and tomorrow's pastries to bake."

"Thanks. If you're sure, I'll do that."

Brenna waved her hand toward the nearly empty seating area. "I can handle this with my eyes closed."

Shelley hung up her apron and put on her coat and gloves. She was bone tired and didn't like to think about the evening ahead of her. At least she'd had the foresight to make extra cookies and some of the best-selling pastries ahead and freeze them, though she preferred to serve fresh-baked. By the end of the week, this schedule could get pretty old. If she'd had to stay and close at six o'clock, she might not have been able to crank out of bed in the morning. And in summer, the Cove stayed open until nine!

She trudged home with her head down and her hands in her pockets. As she left the brighter lights of Main Street behind, she could see that the stars were beginning to pop out. She stopped in at the Hoskins' house, on the off chance that the kids were still there with Adelaide.

"Hi, Shelley," Allan said when he met her at the door. "Dan picked the children up about an hour ago."

"Oh, good. I just thought I'd check. Thanks so much."

"They were very good," Allan said, "and after Hailey got here, they had a ball with Adelaide's old dollhouse."

"That was sweet of Adelaide to let them play with it," Shelley said, knowing how hard Emma could be on toys. "Where is she?"

Allan smiled. "She's in her room now. Do you want to see her?"

"Don't bother her," Shelley said. "I'll head on home. But tell her I said a big thank-you."

She felt grateful anew for her supportive neighbors. Tomorrow, a hired babysitter would stay with Emma all day and be there for Aiden and Hailey during the times they were home, and her father-in-law would make the afternoon school pickups. Tuesday was the only day she'd been able to get someone to agree to a full day. She determined to make the most of it.

She turned toward home and was about to cross the street diagonally when she noticed another figure coming up the sidewalk in the dusk. Beverly had the new puppy on a leash and meandered slowly along.

"Hey," Shelley called. She strode toward her friend, feeling a burst of new energy. "How's the pooch doing?"

Beverly frowned. "*He's* doing fine, but I'm frazzled."

Shelley laughed. "Sorry. I can see you're serious. Did something happen?"

"Nothing major, but all the little things are getting to me. Like now. I just wish he'd do his business so we could go home. But it's cold, and he just wants to go in. That's why I brought him down here. I figured maybe if he got farther from home, he'd quit whining to go back there."

"Well, sometimes their timing isn't the same as ours," Shelley said, glancing beyond Beverly to Diane's house, where a light shone in the study window. "Have you talked to Diane today?"

"Yeah, I spoke to her this afternoon," Beverly said. "She sounded like she was having a good day. She said she'd actually written some on her mystery."

"I'm glad she's getting her energy back," Shelley said. "Come on, I'll walk you home."

"Oh no, you've been over at the Cove all day. You must be anxious to get back to Dan and the kids. We'll walk *you* home."

Shelley fell into step with Beverly, and they crossed the street.

When they gained the sidewalk on the other side, Beverly said, "I'm glad you came along, Shelley. I was feeling pretty tense about this whole dog thing."

"Oh, look," Shelley cried. The pup was indeed "doing his duty."

"Whew!" Beverly said. "Thanks, Shelley."

"Me? I didn't do anything."

"I think you helped me untie a few knots in my stomach." Shelley smiled. "In that case, happy to help." The puppy came over and sniffed the toes of her boots. "He's a cute little scamp."

"Yeah, you're right." Beverly jerked her chin up and fixed Shelley with an intense stare. "Don't you dare tell anyone I said that, will you?"

Shelley laughed. "What, you don't want your dad to hear you're getting soft on the puppy?"

"Something like that. I guess I still have some issues to work through. Me and Mrs. Peabody. Father loves this runt."

"Okay, I won't tell anyone. See ya!" Shelley waved and hurried up her driveway. At the door, she turned to look back. Beverly and the pup had crossed back to their own side of the street and were heading home.

Shelley opened the door.

"Mama!" Emma came toddling toward her, and Aiden ran over with a toy truck in his hand.

"Yay! Mom's home!"

Shelley grinned as she took off her mittens and unwound her scarf. "Hey! Did you have a good time with Adelaide?"

While the little ones regaled her with tales of their activities, Dan and Hailey came out of the kitchen. Shelley smiled at them.

"Something smells good."

"Spaghetti," Dan said. "I used the frozen meatballs. Is that okay?"

"It's great. Thank you both. It's a treat not to have to come home and fix supper."

"Hailey made the salad," Dan said.

"Wonderful. Thanks, Hailey."

Her niece smiled and shrugged. "It wasn't hard. And Uncle Dan let me use the sharp slicing knife. Hey, have you ever seen Adelaide's dollhouse?"

They all went into the kitchen, where Dan and Hailey had set the table almost correctly. Shelley sat down, once more full of thanks but wondering what they would eat for supper tomorrow night. If she decided to work full-time, she'd have to give more thought to the menus for the meals at home—and her shopping trips too.

After the meal, Dan offered to put Emma to bed. Shelley was glad—she was too tired to move, and yet she had to. Even with her remaining freezer stash, she still needed to make fresh muffins for tomorrow, and she ought to do up another flavor of scones; she only had two dozen cinnamon left for the Cove, and they wouldn't last long. She enlisted Hailey's help in loading the dishwasher and then started mixing her batter.

As she set the timer on the first batch of muffins, Dan came into the kitchen.

"Emma's down. I told Aiden and Hailey they could finish their video. It's got about another half hour."

Shelley didn't usually allow television on school nights. She looked at the clock. "Okay. Did Hailey finish her math?"

"Yeah, she showed it to me. It looked okay to me."

Shelley nodded. "As soon as I clean up a little, I'll come sit with you guys for a few minutes. I feel like I've hardly seen anyone all day. Anyone in the family, I mean. Hey, can you stop on your way home tomorrow and pick up some milk and hamburger?"

"Sure. Maybe you'd better put a note in my lunch box, though, so I don't forget." Dan bent to kiss her. "So, what do you think, after your first day?"

"I think I'm really tired. Is this what you feel like every day when you get home?"

He chuckled. "Some days. But I'm not standing up all day."

"Yeah, my feet hurt." Shelley wiggled her toes inside her sneakers.

"Do you want a hot bath?" he asked.

"That sounds great in theory, but since I have to get up superearly again tomorrow, I think I'll settle for a shower when the last batch of muffins comes out and take the extra half hour of sleep instead."

CHAPTER THIRTEEN

Beverly went to the mayor's office on Tuesday morning. To her surprise, Lionel Riley had left a two-page memo on her desk with notes he had made on the town's annual budget. He had agreed to a couple of her suggestions and incorporated them into his figures. In addition, he had come up with another place where they could potentially save a few hundred dollars.

She read his memo thoroughly, checked his figures on her calculator, and sat back with a smile. This was a good start. She picked up the telephone receiver and called him.

"Mr. Riley, this is Beverly Wheeland. I just wanted to thank you for your hard work on the budget proposal."

"Oh well...I should have a more complete file for you in a few weeks."

"There's plenty of time," Beverly said. "And thank you for pointing out that we didn't spend the entire allocation for ballot clerks this year. I believe you're right—with that surplus in hand, we may be able to lower the allocation for next year slightly."

"Well, thank you, mayor." He sounded pleased that she had noticed his contribution, and that she liked his idea.

She spent the next hour looking into ideas she'd had for making the town even more tourist-friendly. The final item to hold her attention that morning was a notice from real-estate agent Patricia Finley that she had just closed a deal on a commercial building on lower Main Street. The new owner hoped to open a seasonal ice cream parlor by Memorial Day, and rent out office or studio space on the upper level.

Beverly typed an e-mail to Patricia, thanking her for the information and encouraging her to invite the new owner to join the local chamber of commerce.

The morning's work satisfied Beverly, and she once more put on her cold-weather gear. She had a half hour or so before she needed to be home for lunch. Since she hadn't seen much of Margaret lately, she decided to walk over to the gallery for a few minutes.

As she approached the door of the Shearwater, Nicole Wharburton was coming out.

"Hello," Beverly said.

"Hello, Mayor Wheeland."

Beverly went inside and found Margaret alone, going over a list at the checkout counter.

"Hi, Beverly. How nice to see you."

"Thanks," Beverly said. "How are you doing?"

"Not too badly. Nicole was just here for her painting lesson. Not many customers came in this morning, but that's all right—we had an almost uninterrupted lesson."

"That's great," Beverly said, although she suspected that Margaret would have preferred brisker sales.

"Well now, how's your little Valentine bundle?" Margaret asked.

"What? Oh, the puppy." Beverly couldn't keep her face from skewing.

"That bad?" Margaret chuckled. "I'm sorry, but there's a modicum of comfort in knowing I wasn't the only one who had an awful Valentine's Day."

"Oh, don't feel bad. Allan is a good sport. It sounded as if your evening turned out all right."

"It did, but…" Margaret shook her head. "I have *got* to learn to cook a meal, even if it's only *one* meal. I need to make it come out right, just one time. Is that silly?"

"Not at all. I've always envied those women who put on a huge Thanksgiving spread for their families and have twenty dishes ready at the same time."

"I would never in a million years be able to do that." Margaret sighed.

"I wish I could help you." Beverly stopped as a sudden thought occurred to her. "Maybe someone else could, though."

"Who?"

"Your art student, Nicole. I was talking to her once— maybe the day they built the Lobster Trap Christmas Tree? Well, anyway, it doesn't matter when. I'm sure she told me she'd had some training several years ago at Le Cordon Bleu."

"Seriously? In Paris?"

"I think so."

"Was she planning a career as a chef?"

Beverly searched her memory for more details. "I don't think so. I believe it was before she went to law school. She was in Paris and decided to take a course there for fun."

Margaret's jaw dropped. "She's never mentioned that to me. How could I not know that?"

"You might want to ask her. Maybe you could trade cooking lessons for art lessons."

"Yeah! That's a great idea. Thanks," Margaret said as the door opened, accompanied by the jingle of the bell that hung on it.

Beverly glanced over her shoulder. Allan entered and quickly closed the door behind him.

"Hello, Beverly," he said.

"Hi, Allan!"

He smiled at Margaret. "I'm just on my way home from the lumber store, and I thought I'd stop by and see if you needed any help."

"No, it's been quite slow this morning, but thanks," Margaret said.

"Okay. Well, if you want a break with Beverly..."

"We could go next door and get some coffee from Shelley," Beverly said. Immediately she felt foolish. Margaret had a full coffeepot and a selection of Shelley's cookies right here in the gallery. But her friend seized upon the idea.

"I'd like that." Margaret turned to her husband. "Allan, do you mind? We'd only be a few minutes. I've been wondering how Shelley's doing."

"Sure, go ahead," Allan said.

Margaret hurried to the back room for her coat, hat, and gloves. Soon she and Beverly were outside, walking the few yards between the gallery's front door and the Cove's.

Her first impression was that the coffee shop was far busier than Margaret's gallery. At least ten people sat at tables, and two more stood at the counter, getting their drinks.

When it was their turn to order, Shelley grinned at them. "Well, hey! Who's holding things down next door?"

"Allan is," Margaret replied. "How are you?"

"Great," Shelley said. "Brenna and I have got a routine down, and we work well together. It's kind of fun. It's chaotic for the first hour or two in the morning, though. There's this big rush of people who come in on their way to their jobs. If you've never seen it, you might not believe it!"

"The side of Marble Cove we slugabeds never see," Margaret said with a chuckle. "I'd like a caramel latte, please."

Brenna came over to the counter. "Hello, Mayor! Hi, Mrs. Hoskins."

They greeted her, and Beverly gave her order for regular coffee. She didn't want to have anything sweet so close to lunch. They took a small table, and Shelley came over to talk to them for a few minutes. When more customers entered, she went back to help Brenna serve them.

"She seems to be doing all right," Beverly said.

Margaret nodded. "Shelley's a smart girl. I figured she'd land on her feet. But I think she's experiencing the harsh reality of working outside the home too."

"Yes. This should help her make her decision." Beverly finished her coffee and glanced at her watch. If she left now, she would have time to take the puppy out for a few minutes before lunch. "I should go. Mrs. Peabody hates to serve lunch late."

"I don't want to impose too long on Allan either," Margaret said.

They stepped out into the sharp, cold air. Beverly turned toward Newport Avenue, and Margaret back toward the Shearwater. Beverly hoped her suggestion of culinary help worked out for Margaret. Now to go home and find out what mischief the puppy had wreaked in her absence.

* * *

Diane's phone rang while she was removing her boots. She'd had Rocky out for a short stint on the beach, and now she hoped to spend some time on her blog. She had gone over her idea for her new post while she walked, and she wanted to get right at it.

Caller ID told her it was Leo. She hadn't seen him since Saturday, when Martin had arrived so unexpectedly. She found that she actually looked forward to talking to her friend again.

"Hi, Leo!"

"Well, hi," he said. "You sound cheerful today."

"I'm feeling pretty good. And Rocky and I just had a walk on the beach."

"*Brr.*"

She smiled. "Yeah, it was chilly. A little breezy today, so we didn't stay out long."

"How's the computer doing?" Leo asked. "I thought I'd check in and see if it's behaving for you."

"It's been fine ever since you straightened it out. Thanks again."

"No problem," he said. "How's the book coming?"

"Not bad. I've been puttering at it for the last few days. I want to put a new post on my blog this afternoon, and then I need to go pick up a prescription, but I did do a little bit on the book this morning."

"Would it help if I got the prescription for you?" Leo asked. "I'm closing the office at four today, and I could pick it up if you like."

Diane hesitated. While it was true that she felt more energetic than she had a few days ago, she was also a bit tired from the exercise she'd just had, and she would have to take Rocky out again later. Leo's offer would save her the strain of a car trip to the pharmacy and waiting while they got her order ready.

"You know, I think that would be nice, if you're sure."

"Absolutely," Leo said. "I'll pick it up and bring it to you around four thirty or five."

"Great. I'll give the pharmacy a call and let them know it's all right for you to get it."

Knowing Leo would come by later spurred her to action, and for the next twenty minutes she bustled about, straightening the living room, emptying the kitchen trash, and washing the few dishes she had left in the sink. By the time she was ready to sit down at her desk, she was puffing.

"Okay, Diane, stop it," she told herself. "Leo does not expect your house to be immaculate. If you wear yourself out cleaning, what's the point of having him go to the drugstore for you?"

Rocky yipped and cocked his head to one side.

Diane laughed and patted his head. "You're right, boy. I'm talking to myself. It's okay when I talk to you, right? But when I talk to myself...Well, just let me know if I start answering back, okay?"

She went to the refrigerator and poured herself a glass of juice, which she carried into the study. Time to get going on that blog post, before she forgot all the points she wanted to make.

Soon she was immersed in reading new comments left on her previous post and answering each one. Afterward she felt that the topic she'd been mulling on her walk—accepting a new level of energy and performance after illness—was more appropriate than ever. She spent an hour writing and rewriting what she wanted to say and finally posted the piece.

Once again she had let lunchtime pass her by, a bad habit she needed to work on. Her hypoglycemia was reason enough to keep a regular meal schedule, but she was also trying to rebuild from her cancer siege. Now that she could stay in all afternoon, she would pamper herself a little.

She made a nourishing lunch of vegetable soup and a sandwich and then lay down for a short rest. To make sure she wouldn't sleep until Leo's arrival and have to greet him groggy and bleary-eyed, she set the alarm for four, but she woke from her nap an hour before that. In fact, by the time he arrived, she had done a satisfying amount of research that would help her move her new novel ahead.

When Leo rang her doorbell at four thirty, she was ready for another break and some company. She opened the door to find him holding the small white bag from the pharmacy.

"Thanks so much, Leo," she said. "I was about to have a cup of tea. Will you join me?"

"Uh, sure." He seemed surprised and pleased.

"I ate lunch late, so I'm just going to have a little snack now and eat dinner later," she explained. "Tea, coffee, or hot chocolate?"

"Tea is fine," he said. "Whatever you're having."

While the tea water heated, she brought out her cell phone. "Beverly Wheeland has a new puppy, and I took some pictures of him the other day with Rocky. They're so cute! You have to see these."

She opened the photo archive and handed him the phone. "There are about a half-dozen pictures."

Leo laughed as he clicked through them. "Cute little guy. It's a schnoodle, right?"

"Yes." Diane laughed and told him what Beverly had said about naming the puppy. "I'm not sure whether she's come up with anything or not."

"Maybe she's still calling him 'Down Boy,' do you think?"

"Could be." Diane took their mugs to the table. They chatted easily while they sipped their tea.

"Well, I guess I'd better shove off," Leo said when he'd drained his cup a few minutes later. "Limo will be waiting for his turn to go out."

"Thanks so much for getting the pills for me."

"Glad to do it." He smiled warmly as he zipped his jacket.

Rocky went with them to the door, and Leo paused to stroke the dog for a moment. "You take good care of Diane, fella," he said.

Diane watched him get into his car and waved. As she closed the door, she reflected on how comfortable she'd felt with Leo today—more like she had during the time they spent together over the holidays.

She looked down at Rocky, who was eyeing her hopefully, his tail swaying back and forth.

"I suppose we may as well go out now," she said. "It's already getting dark." As she opened the coat closet to get her jacket, Rocky barked and leaped forward. Diane laughed. "Okay, but I warn you, I'm not staying out there long. I just got another idea, and I want to do some more writing tonight."

★ ★ ★

Beverly smacked her temple lightly with her palm as she surveyed the kitchen floor. "Oh no. Did you have to?"

Her father called from the dining room, "What's the matter?"

"He did it again. Right in front of the refrigerator. And I just had him outside an hour ago."

Her father's slow footsteps advanced, and he said from the doorway, "He's only a baby."

She laughed. "Sure. I heard you telling him what a big boy he is this afternoon."

"It's all a matter of perspective and timing, I guess."

"Right." She let out a big sigh. "No point in taking him out now. Can you put him in his crate while I clean up?"

"Come on, Junior."

Beverly gritted her teeth and refrained from commenting on the nickname. She really had to think of something to call that mutt.

A few minutes later, her father came back to the kitchen. "Anything I can do to help?"

"No," she said. "I'm almost finished. I just need to disinfect." She straightened and let out a big puff of breath. "I don't know what possessed Jeff to do this to me."

"He has no idea. He thought it was a good thing, and that you'd love the little guy."

"I know, but"—she shook her head—"how can he be so clueless? About me, I mean. We're getting married. How can he not know I don't like dogs?" Tears filled her eyes, and she tried to fight them back. "Pets are so…unpredictable."

"Spoken like a very organized person who's uncomfortable when her routine is interrupted." Her father walked over and placed a gentle hand on her shoulder. "Maybe you should tell him how you feel."

She shook her head, knowing she couldn't bring herself to do that. "I'll manage. Somehow. I keep telling myself it will get better."

"When's Jeff coming here again?"

"Not until next week anyway."

"*Hmm.*"

She glared at him. "What does that mean?"

"Nothing—just thinking. My dear girl, you really need to come to terms with this before you see Jeff again. If you can't handle it—"

"I can handle it," she insisted, wiping a tear off her cheek. She hated that she'd shown her frustration, even to her father.

"Okay," he said. "I'm going to put the teakettle on while you disinfect the floor."

Beverly went to the laundry room, where they kept most of the cleaning supplies. As she opened the cupboard, she noticed that a few items had fallen out of the basket of dirty laundry in the corner. Or had they fallen? Maybe someone had pulled them out. She picked up a hand towel and held it up for inspection. As she'd feared, since yesterday a large hole had appeared in it. She stooped for one of her father's socks—also chewed. Ruined. Apparently the little monster preferred their laundry to toys and rawhide chews.

Too exasperated to deal with the matter, she dropped the sock and the towel, took the disinfectant from the cupboard, and went out, firmly closing the laundry room door.

Chapter Fourteen

On Wednesday afternoon, Beverly headed for the historical society. She'd been putting the visit off far too long. The temperature had climbed to a balmy forty degrees, and she decided to walk.

On Main Street, she saw Margaret leaving the gallery and called to her.

"Oh, hi," Margaret said. "I'm heading to the community center for a tai chi class. Where are you off to?"

"The library—I'm hoping to find something that will justify designating the old train station as a historical landmark."

"Good," Margaret said. "That seems to me the best way to keep Dennis Calder from tearing it down."

"We'll see." Beverly wasn't at all sure they could turn up enough evidence.

Once she reached the old brick building, she went upstairs to the Maine Room. The Marble Cove Historical Society housed its book collection here, and she turned to the old, out-of-print volumes with information on Maine's coastal region.

She sat down with a likely-looking book and was soon engrossed in the fascinating information. After half an hour, she realized she was allowing herself to be sidetracked by historical anecdotes and needed to focus on finding more about the town's industry.

Finally she found a nugget, at the end of the section on transportation. Railroad service to Marble Cove had ended in March 1952. She made a note and then looked for other, more specific books. While nothing targeted the 1950s, she did find a town history written in the 1970s, and she figured it might have more information.

After careful scrutiny, she found a paragraph stating that Elias Thorpe, the last stationmaster, had left town on the last train. The author then wrote, "So far as is known, Mr. Thorpe never returned to Marble Cove, and residents are mystified as to what became of him."

Beverly frowned and read it again. Interesting, but they already knew all that. She wrote down the title of the book and the author's name. Maybe Augie Jackson knew the person who wrote the book, and they could contact her and talk to her directly to see if she had any clues, however sketchy, that they could follow up on.

She checked the index of both of the volumes she had referenced to see if there were any other mentions of Elias Thorpe or the quarry, but had no success in that vein. She did, however, find the name of Otto William Frederickson in another book's index. A few months previously, she and her friends had learned that Frederickson was the architect who had designed the railroad depot. She turned to the page with his name and read more, discovering that he had also designed a church in Rockland, an Art Deco movie theater and a courthouse in another county, and other landmark buildings around the region. Maybe he was famous enough to help build their case for listing the railroad station as a historical landmark.

She decided to copy the page about Frederickson and see if the librarian had any ideas that would help her. Gilda Harris was behind the counter sorting books to be reshelved. Beverly greeted her and told her that she was looking for information about the train station and the quarry, or anything to do with Elias Thorpe.

"*Hmm*," Gilda said, peeping at her over the rim of her reading glasses. "I almost think there was an article about the Burr Oak Quarry in an old magazine. Oh, and several of the regional magazines have done articles over the years on the short railroad lines and the narrow gauge. But you know, there was one that ceased publishing twenty or thirty years ago. I do think they did one on the limestone quarries, and it had some details about our quarry. We've got most of their issues in the archives. Hold on a sec."

Gilda went to the nearest computer terminal and clicked away for several seconds. "Okay, here we are. I'll get it for you."

When Gilda returned with it, Beverly took the magazine and went back up to the quiet Maine room. She sat in a padded rocker near the window and opened to the article on limestone and marble quarrying in the coastal region. She found the article quite interesting and decided to copy it so she could share it with her friends.

The most intriguing thing, to her mind, was a hint of financial misdeeds and corruption in connection with the Burr Oak Quarry in Marble Cove. The quarry had shut down in November 1951, so Beverly made a note to recheck the *Courier* morgue for issues published around that time. She thought about how the closing might have affected the stationmaster, who was also an investor in the quarry business. Did his disappearance a few months later have to do with the scandal at the quarry?

Resigned to having to revisit the dusty *Courier* archives to learn more, Beverly took the magazine downstairs and photocopied the article, then returned the issue to Gilda.

"Find anything?" Gilda's blue eyes twinkled.

"Yes," Beverly said, "some history and a little speculation. Thanks a lot."

★ ★ ★

"Are you sure you wouldn't mind?" Margaret clutched the phone and scanned her calendar. "Wonderful. Tomorrow is fine for me. I'll come to your house right after I close the gallery. Thanks so much, Nicole."

A quartet of customers came in two middle aged married couples she knew slightly. One of the wives had bought a high-end painting from Margaret the previous year. She signed off with Nicole and hung up, unable to suppress a grin. Her cooking lessons would begin tomorrow, only a week after her huge disaster. This was progress!

"Good afternoon," she said cheerfully as she walked toward the newcomers. "It's good to see you folks."

Two hours later she closed for the day, still feeling euphoric. She had sold another painting, the first large sale in over two weeks. And Allan would be happy to hear that one of the ladies had purchased two of his walnut candlesticks. She found that his larger items like inlaid tables sold best when the summer tourists thronged the town, but smaller pieces continued to sell through the winter, often as gifts.

Today was one of Adelaide's afternoons to mind Hailey and the Bauer children, and this time she had gone to Shelley and Dan's house with the assurance that both Allan and Diane were at home just across the street if she needed any help. Allan had also promised to check in midway through Adelaide's time with the children.

Dan's pickup was just pulling into the Bauers' driveway when she got there, and Margaret drove in and parked right behind him.

"Hi, Dan," she called, getting out of the car. "You managed to get off early, I see."

"Yup, it worked out fine today. Our job was in Willow Corners."

She and Dan went into the house together. Adelaide had apparently heard them coming, as she had the three children scrambling about the living room to pick up blocks and action figures and put them in a plastic bin.

"Hi, Mom!" Adelaide's face glowed. "Hi, Dan. We built a town."

"Did you?" Dan asked, obviously amused.

"It's messy," Adelaide admitted, tossing a block into the bin.

"That's okay," Dan said. "It looks like everyone's cooperating to clean up."

"Did the children behave well?" Margaret asked her.

"Uh-huh. And when Aiden and Hailey came home, we had the snack Shelley showed me when she left."

"That sounds just right, honey," Margaret said. Shelley had apprised her of the plan for her mother-in-law to keep Emma that morning and make sure Adelaide felt comfortable with her duties before she left.

"Mr. Allan came over too," Aiden said. "He brought us grapes."

"Aha." Dan smiled at Margaret over Aiden's head.

"Dad didn't stay though," Adelaide told them. "He said he had work to do and we were doing fine."

"Yup, we were just fine," Aiden put in.

Hailey, who had kept busy picking up toys, came over and stood before Dan. "We're finished, Uncle Dan. Can we make supper now?"

"Sounds as though everything's under control and we should skedaddle," Margaret said. "Adelaide, do you have everything?"

"I think so." Her daughter was pulling on her gloves.

Margaret waited for her to zip her coat and pick up the tote bag she'd brought with her. Once they were in the car,

Margaret started the engine and said, "Two very nice things happened to me today."

"You sold a painting," Adelaide said immediately.

Margaret smiled. "Yes, I did. That's one of them. And you can tell Dad about it if you want. But the other one's a secret for us."

"Okay," Adelaide said doubtfully.

"Mrs. Wharburton—the lady who's taking painting lessons from me—is going to teach me to cook."

"Really?" Adelaide still looked dubious, and Margaret had to laugh.

"Are you thinking of the special Valentine dinner that I ruined?"

Adelaide nodded.

"So was I. Then I found out Mrs. Wharburton is an expert cook, and so I'm trading off with her—she'll give me cooking lessons instead of paying for her next few art lessons."

"That's good, I guess."

"I think it's good," Margaret said, pulling into their driveway, "but don't mention that part to Dad, all right? You can tell him about your afternoon with the kids and the painting. The one I sold was the nighttime lighthouse one that was in the front part of the gallery."

"I like that one."

"So do I, but I'm glad the customers liked it too. I can paint another one that we'll like just as much."

* * *

"You're late heading home," Beverly said as she entered the kitchen.

To her chagrin, Mrs. Peabody was bent over, hand feeding a bit of food to the puppy.

"What's this?"

Mrs. Peabody straightened quickly and turned away. "Just a bit of leftover chicken. It'll be getting dark soon."

Beverly's jaw dropped. Now the persnickety housekeeper was giving the dog treats. After all of Mrs. Peabody's complaints about the pup, Beverly wouldn't have believed it if she hadn't seen it with her own eyes. She was starting to feel outnumbered.

The older woman placidly removed her apron and hung it on a hook beside the refrigerator. "Guess I'd best be getting home."

"I'll walk with you," Beverly said. She worried about Mrs. Peabody sometimes in the winter. A man came after every storm to clear the woman's driveway and walk, but even so, it would be easy for her to slip and fall, and no one else would be there to help her. Beverly and her father tried to remember to at least watch out the window when she left, to be sure she got home safely.

"I'll be fine," Mrs. Peabody said, jutting her chin out.

"I'm sure you will, but the puppy needs to go out, and I'd as soon do it now as after dark. Let us see you home."

They both bundled up, and Beverly told her father where she was going. The trio left the house with Mrs. Peabody easing slowly down the steps while clutching the railing and the little gray pup straining at the leash to get out into the snow and play.

Across the street, Mr. Calder's house nestled cozily with a blanket of snow on the roof. A light was on in his front room. Mrs. Peabody's lavender Victorian stood proud and regal, and Beverly noted that she had left the porch light on—not a bad idea in this season of early twilight. On the other side, the empty Simpson house, where renters often stayed in summer, was dark and bleak, with its driveway unplowed.

They walked across the street slowly, with Beverly watching toward the corner for traffic coming in off Main Street, but no vehicles came along to disturb their progress. A layer of snow crunched underfoot in the driveway. Mrs. Peabody used the railing to help pull herself up the front steps. She was still spry for a woman in her eighties, but she had just spent several hours at the Wheeland house, much of it on her feet.

"You could take tomorrow off if you want to," Beverly said.

Mrs. Peabody snorted. "Why would I want to do that?"

"To rest, maybe?" Beverly realized she'd taken the wrong approach and inadvertently insulted her. "I just meant that if you ever want to take some time off, we can get by on our own for a day or two."

Mrs. Peabody eyed her keenly and reached for the doorknob. "I'll let you know if I start feeling poorly."

"Good," Beverly said, striving for a cheerful note. "We appreciate what you do for us so much—and today's Italian chicken was scrumptious." *Even the dog thought so,* she told herself, but didn't hint of her displeasure out loud.

"Your father needs a good, balanced diet."

"Oh yes, indeed he does. Well, I'll see you tomorrow then."

"Good night," Mrs. Peabody said. She went inside and shut the door firmly. A light came on in the front hall, shining out through the sidelights next to the door.

Beverly tugged the leash gently. "Come on, little guy. We'd best get down these steps before she shuts off the porch light."

When they reached the sidewalk, the puppy had not yet settled down to accomplish the purpose for the walk, so Beverly headed toward the shore, passing the Simpson house. As they walked on toward the Bauers', she tried not to let the resentment inside her foment. Some days, she felt as though everyone was against her—at home anyway. Things seemed to be going fairly well at the municipal building and in her business relationships. But a cloud hung over her at home.

It all centered on the puppy. She knew that. She still begrudged Jeff for dumping this animal on her. And her father hadn't soothed her injured spirit by taking to the dog immediately. He actually seemed to like it when the puppy climbed in his lap. Beverly couldn't stand that. All toenails and tousled hair, the pup seemed to think all humans liked nothing better than having their faces licked. And then there were the items he'd ruined with his chewing. The list grew longer every day. She found it incredible that Mrs. Peabody had let him go into the kitchen today. Instead of throwing him out with a scorching lecture, she'd fed him a bit of chicken!

Beverly shook her head. They were all against her.

CHAPTER FIFTEEN

I never thought of writing out a schedule," Margaret said, frowning in concentration over her notepad.

Nicole smiled. "It's a great help when you're planning a complicated meal. It will even show you things you can prepare ahead of time, and you'll know what has to be done at the last minute, like tearing the salad greens. Now, write down that when you take out the chicken you'll turn up the oven temperature, and five minutes later, you'll slide the rolls in the oven."

"What about the dessert?" Margaret asked.

"That will be baked. You'll make it the night before."

"But don't we want to warm it up while we're eating the main course?"

"That's where your microwave can help. Bake your fruit crisp in a glass pan, and you can heat it in the microwave."

"That's so simple. Why didn't I think of that?"

"Because it's not your usual province." Nicole's oven timer rang, and she touched Margaret's sleeve. "What's next? Check your list."

When Margaret reached home at suppertime, her head was spinning with cooking instructions. She'd made a wonderful, spongy roll dough that Nicole assured her was perfect. She hadn't been able to stay through the second rising, though. And the mixed berry crisp, while a more humble dessert than the one she had tried to make for Valentine's Day, was also easier to prepare. Nicole had assured her that the recipe was foolproof, and had showed her how to dress it up with a garnish of low-fat ice cream and flaked chocolate. Another point that pleased Margaret was that the new menu was lower in fat than her old one, a plus for Allan's heart condition.

When she arrived at home, Allan had supper ready, and Adelaide was laying the silverware on the table.

"Hi," he said. "You're a little late today."

Adelaide grinned. "Mom had her class with Mrs. Wharburton."

Margaret's heart lurched.

"Really?" Allan asked. "I didn't think this was the day for her painting lesson."

"It's not usually," Margaret said quickly, throwing her daughter a sharp glance. "We got busy and lost track of time. Sorry." She hoped she could get by with that explanation. Allan wasn't one to nitpick.

"No harm," he said. "It's only spaghetti tonight."

Adelaide's face bore a look of contrition. Now, if only she could keep quiet and not start apologizing, things would be fine.

Margaret quickly took off her outerwear. While she washed her hands, she said, "I sold some of Bernadette's jewelry today." She hoped that by changing the subject, she could keep Adelaide from spilling the beans before she was ready to wow Allan with her new skills. Another week should do it. Adelaide tended to get very excited about new things, especially secrets, and sometimes she forgot from whom she was supposed to keep the secret. Margaret almost wished she hadn't told her. On the other hand, it was fun to have someone rooting for her, and sharing it with Adelaide had boosted her own spirits. Perhaps another private talk would do the trick—a gentle reminder that this was a surprise for Dad. Surely they could keep this secret a little while longer.

★ ★ ★

Shelley scuttled back and forth between the counter and kitchen area at the Cove. She had thought she could get away with baking only one kind of cookies last night, but the fierce morning run on muffins and scones had left them with low supplies, and by 9:00 AM she was baking in the Cove's kitchen while Parker manned the counter.

Whenever she could, she dashed out to refill the coffeepots and help him for a few minutes. She knew Parker hated to put new gloves on every time he handled food and take them off again to receive money. So far he'd gone through about half a box of disposable gloves. Having one do the food while the other tended the cash register was much more efficient. With a sigh, she resolved to do some major baking at home tonight, no matter how tired she felt.

The phone rang, and Parker yelled, "Shelley, it's for you!"

She snatched a tray of cranberry scones from the oven and set it on a cooking rack before she went to take the call.

"Hey," Dan said. "How's it going?"

"Not too bad." She lifted her apron and dabbed at her damp forehead. "How are the kids doing?"

"Well, it's just Emma now, and she's fussing some. She really misses you."

Shelley's heart wrenched.

"And Aiden couldn't find one of his mittens this morning," Dan added. "I made him wear that old blue pair, but he was upset when he left. How do you do this every day?"

Shelley laughed. "It's a challenge."

"Well, I called because I just talked to Wayne. He really needs me tomorrow."

"Oh no." Shelley's frustration roared into action. Dan had arranged to have both Thursday and Friday off.

"I know, but he's got a chance for a new job, and we have to start tomorrow. It's a good one that would keep us going for at least three weeks. But he needs to show up with a full crew."

"Okay." Shelley knew Wayne had been very accommodating to allow Dan even one day off this week. She rapidly ran down a mental list of babysitters. "Adelaide can't come tomorrow. What about your mom?"

"She's sick. I talked to her earlier, and she sounds terrible. I don't think you want the kids around her for a few days."

"Right. Let me think about it."

"What about your friend Allie?" Dan asked.

"No, she's working full-time now. I guess you'll have to start making some calls. We're pretty busy here."

"Where do I start?"

Shelley thought for a moment. "Try your sisters first, I guess. If you could drop Emma at Annie's—"

"I have to leave here by seven in the morning to meet Wayne on time."

Shelley sighed. The noise level in the coffee shop seemed to have increased. She looked over her shoulder to see that Parker was besieged by patrons.

"I really need to go. I'm sorry. Maybe I can get Brenna to open in the morning, if I stay late tomorrow, but that isn't even close to being my first choice. Call your sisters— and possibly Diane could drop Aiden and Hailey at school in the morning. I'd hate to ask her, but it's a last-resort option."

"Okay, talk to you later," Dan said.

Shelley ran to the kitchen to throw a pan of muffins into the oven and take the cooled scones off the tray. She plunged back into the work at the counter, but her mind stewed on the child-care problem. The kids' safety was crucial. How did single moms ever manage?

Dan didn't call back until almost one o'clock. Brenna had come in before lunch and was now manning the cash register.

"Okay, this is what I've got," Dan said, in an I-dare-you-to-tell-me-it-won't-work tone. "Annie will be here by seven. She'll drive Aiden and Hailey to school and then take Emma to her house. But she'll have to keep her all day. She has something at her church in the afternoon, but she said she could take Emma with her."

"What kind of thing?" Shelley asked. "Would Emma be in the nursery, or what?"

"I don't know." Dan sounded more and more irritated.

"And what about Aiden and Hailey?"

"That girl you had the other day—Liddy—she'll come after school."

"Liddy? Oh, Dan, I don't know."

"Now, listen," he insisted. "I told her I'd leave the key in the mailbox for her. Shelley, come on. She did all right, didn't she?"

"Yes, but she's only fourteen, Dan."

He sighed. "That's old enough to babysit. And we've had her before."

"Yes. All right. When can she get there?"

"Her bus can drop her at the corner around three."

"So she ought to be there when Hailey finishes for the day, but what about Aiden? He gets done a little earlier, and who will bring them home?"

"That's the tricky part. Diane said she'll get Aiden. He can stay at her house until Allan gets home, which should be between two and two thirty. Allan will pick up Hailey and then get Aiden from Diane and keep him and Hailey until Liddy gets here."

Shelley's jaw dropped. "That's insane."

"Babe, it will work," Dan said.

The timer bell on the oven rang. "I need to go," Shelley said. "Look, you did a great job, but we need to try to smooth that timeline out a little if we can. I'll talk to you later."

She flitted about the Cove's kitchen, badly distracted from her work. Dan's cobbled-together plan was full of weak links. If one person failed her children…

Brenna popped her head around the corner. "The afternoon coffee-break crowd is here en masse. Can you help out front?"

"Be right with you," Shelley called.

* * *

The clouds thickened over the shoreline on Thursday afternoon. Beverly had driven to Portland that morning for a two-hour meeting with one of her corporate clients. It had not gone as smoothly as she'd hoped. She would have to spend a couple of days reworking some of her projections for them. On the way home, she had gotten behind a slow-moving truck on a road where she had no chance to pass. At last, she turned onto Newport Avenue, ready to unwind. She was just entering the house when her cell phone rang.

She quickly peeled off her coat and glanced at the screen. Jeff was calling. His latest assignment had taken him to Cape Cod, and she hoped he was back in Maine.

"Hi," she said, pulling off her hat with her free hand. Part of her brain registered that the house smelled of damp dog.

"Hello. How's it going?"

"Oh, not bad," she said.

"Just not bad? You sound a little glum," Jeff said. "Does it help to know I'm back in Portland?"

She frowned. "Not a whole lot. I just came from there."

"No! Really? I'm sorry. I should have called you last night. We could have arranged to have lunch together today. What does your weekend look like?"

"They're predicting a heavy snowstorm. In fact, a few flakes were coming down just now, when I drove home."

"*Hmm*, guess we'd better play it by ear. Maybe things will clear up by Saturday."

"I hope so," Beverly said.

"So, how's the puppy doing?" Jeff asked.

Beverly sighed. "Well...I just don't know about this, Jeff."

"What do you mean?"

She wished she hadn't said anything. She was tired, and this wasn't a good time to get into it.

"Nothing," she said.

"No, come on. It's something. What's wrong?"

"I just—well, he chews on everything. He's ruined Father's slippers and an afghan and Mrs. Peabody's oven mitt. Several socks and a hand towel...it's just getting frustrating. And we have to keep taking him out all the time—'we' meaning me." She needed to stop talking. She could hear the beginnings of a whine in her voice.

"Is he training okay on that?" Jeff asked.

"Depends on what you call okay. He's had three accidents in the house—no, four. I forgot about the last one. It's just...well, like I said, it's frustrating."

"I'm sorry," Jeff said. "Can I help?"

"I don't see how. You're not home enough to take care of him at your place."

"Well, no. But I thought you and your dad would like having him."

Beverly clamped her mouth shut. Several retorts came to mind, and probably the best she could do at that moment was to keep silent.

"Beverly?" Jeff asked cautiously. "What are you saying? Do you want to get rid of the puppy?"

"No, Jeff, I'm just saying that it would have been nice if you'd asked me first."

There. It was out. She looked up in time to see her father standing in the doorway with his jaw gaping. Great. Now he knew she'd vented at Jeff.

"I...I don't know what to say." His voice sounded contrite over her phone.

"Neither do I. I'm sorry for saying that. Really." She ran a hand through her hair. She wanted to go into the living room and sit down, but she couldn't do that until she had a chance to take off her high leather boots, and she couldn't do that with one hand.

"Look, I'll try to find somebody who'll take him."

"No, don't do that," she snapped.

"Isn't that what you want?"

"No. To be honest, I'm not sure what I want."

"Well, why don't you think about it?" Jeff asked testily. "When you know what you want, clue me in, all right? I'm not a mind reader."

"I already figured that out."

He hung up. She couldn't believe it, but he did.

On second thought, she *could* believe it. She'd been pretty nasty, and now her stomach roiled and her throat tightened. Her eyes filled with tears.

She blinked through them at her father.

"Was that Jeff?" he asked.

She gulped. "Yeah."

"Ouch."

Beverly scowled and shoved her phone into her pocket.

"I've never heard you fight with him before."

"That's because I haven't." She bent over and unzipped the left boot. She wanted to scream, "Leave me alone!" Instead, she took off the boots, set them neatly side by side in the closet, and padded over to the base of the staircase in her stocking feet. "I'll be down in a few minutes to get supper."

As she headed up the stairs, her father said, "Do I dare ask how your trip went?"

She paused and pulled in a deep breath. "Fine. It went just fine."

Carefully, she put one foot ahead of the other and walked up to her room. She shut the door and leaned against it. She hadn't felt so much like screaming in years.

CHAPTER SIXTEEN

Shelley debated whether or not to open the Cove on Friday morning. Snow had fallen through the night, leaving a good eight inches on the ground. Main Street was plowed when she got there at five thirty, but the small parking area was not. Since the Crow's Nest wouldn't open until at least nine, she didn't think the owner would mind if she parked over there until her own space was plowed.

The first thing she did when she got inside was dump her purse and go out back for the shovel. She would do the front entry first. There wasn't much point in shoveling the back door until the parking area was plowed.

Once she had the front cleared so that customers could get in off the sidewalk without thrashing through a snowbank, she leaned the shovel against the wall and went back to her car for the boxes of fresh pastries she'd brought along. By the time she was in the kitchen and starting the coffee, she had only ten minutes left before opening time.

No one's going to come in this morning, she thought. *It's too nasty out.*

She had insisted Dan call his boss at the crack of dawn. Wayne had been firm—they had to start the new job today, or they'd lose it. Shelley hoped their complicated plans for the children's care would hold together.

The front door opened, and she whirled around behind the counter. One of the regulars was walking in grinning. He was the driver for the local heating oil company.

"You open yet?"

"Come on in, Bill," Shelley replied. "I might as well be. What'll you have?"

"Coffee and a blueberry muffin, if you've got 'em today."

"I sure do. I baked a double batch last night. And I just started the coffee, so it'll be a couple of minutes."

So much for the no-shows. She brought him his muffin on a plate and set a clean mug beside the coffeemaker.

"I almost stayed home today," Bill said, "but folks wouldn't appreciate that."

"No, you can't let your customers run out of oil," Shelley said.

By the time the first pot of coffee was ready, two other hardy souls had joined Bill at the counter.

"The snow's let up," one of them said.

"Maybe for the time being," Bill replied, "but I heard we're going to get another foot out of this."

"Oh, I hope not." Shelley brought one of the newcomers a latte and took his payment.

The morning rush wasn't as great as usual, but she still had enough customers to keep her busy. The part-time worker who was scheduled to help her that morning called in to report that she couldn't get out of her driveway. Shelley told her not to worry about it and persevered alone until Brenna arrived.

"It's snowing again," Brenna said cheerfully as she took off her wraps.

"Do you think we should close early?" Shelley asked.

"No, it's not bad right now." Brenna peeked out into the store. "Looks like we've got some traffic."

"Yes, people have been in and out all morning," Shelley said. "Maybe half the usual crowd."

"Well then, let's keep working and put in a full day for Rusty." Brenna pulled her apron on and tied the strings.

"Okay, but I need to move my car over here now that our parking lot is plowed." She went to get her car and found the street sloppy with wet snow. She parked next to Brenna and hurried back in through the rear door of the Cove.

When the snow increased after lunch, Shelley's anxiety set in. She called Diane to check on Aiden.

"Not to worry," Diane said in her soothing voice. "Aiden and I are having a blast."

Shelley exhaled. "Thank you so much. I couldn't believe it when Dan told me the lineup he'd put together for today."

"Well, I'm glad he called me. We've been brushing Rocky, and he's all pretty now. We're going to read a story and have a little snack before Aiden goes to the Hoskins' house."

Shelley decided to take advantage of the sluggish flow of clientele to bake pastries for Saturday. That way she would have less to do at home tonight. Brenna tended the few customers while she made scone dough and rolled it out. As she arranged the first batch on the baking sheet, Brenna let out a little yelp.

"What happened?" Shelley whipped around. She hadn't even been aware that Brenna was in the kitchen.

"I cut myself. I was slicing open a muffin to warm it for someone."

Shelley grabbed a clean dishcloth and ran to Brenna's side. "Is it bad?"

"Kinda."

Brenna's right hand was clamped around her left, but blood oozed out between her fingers.

"Let me see," Shelley said. As soon as she saw the cut, she caught her breath. "Wrap this cloth around it. You need to go to the ER."

"I can't."

"Yes, you can," Shelley said. "If you don't think you can drive yourself, I'll call an ambulance."

"Don't do that," Brenna cried, hugging the clean cloth to her wound.

"How about if I call the fire station? They always have an EMT on duty, don't they?"

"I guess so."

"Sit down." Shelley guided her to a stool. "I'll call and see if one of them can come look at your hand. They can tell you if you need to go to the hospital—but I think you do. You really need stitches."

Tears welled in Brenna's eyes. "You're probably right, but I don't like it. And I don't think I could drive that far in this snow, even if I wasn't bleeding."

"My other option is to close the shop and take you myself," Shelley said.

"No, don't do that. We can't let Rusty down." Brenna sighed. "All right, call the fire station, I guess."

Shelley made the call, then went out front to find four customers waiting for service. While she fixed their orders, she got an impromptu weather report from them—the unrelenting snow was supposed to end by midnight.

When they all had their coffee and food, she told them, "If you need anything, I'll be in the kitchen, so just give me a yell, okay?" Then she scurried to the back to see how Brenna was doing.

"I'm hanging in there," Brenna said. "You'll have to close tonight, though."

"Don't worry about that," Shelley told her. "I've got the list."

Someone rapped loudly on the back door and she rushed to open it. Two firemen stood outside, engulfed in their cold-weather gear. At least they were able to park just outside the back door and not block the street.

The EMT gave Brenna's hand a quick look and said, "Yeah, you need to go in. Since it's snowing so hard, we'll take you in the rescue unit."

"You can do that?" Brenna asked tearfully.

"In a situation like this, yeah. We're not a full ambulance, but we're not going to call for one to come all the way out here on these roads today. We can get you to the hospital quicker than you'd get there if you waited for them anyway."

"Okay," Brenna said. "Let me get my coat."

Shelley brought her purse and her coat. A couple of minutes later, Brenna was out the back door with the firemen. The store was very quiet. Shelley went back to the counter. Only three customers were still in the Cove, drinking their coffee. One man was reading a newspaper. The other two were talking animatedly at one of the back tables.

Shelley considered closing up. What was the point anyway? If she locked up and a couple of people were disappointed, would it matter? A look at the clock told her that she should stay open for two more hours. People who worked in Marble Cove but lived out of town sometimes stopped in for coffee before driving home. She hovered in indecision and then picked up her phone.

"Hello?" came Hailey's tentative voice.

"Hi, honey. It's Aunt Shelley. How're things?"

"Well…"

Shelley's heart leaped to her throat. "Is something wrong?"

"Liddy had to go home."

"What?"

"Her dad came and got her. He wouldn't wait around because of the snow."

"You're kidding!" Shelley's legs felt weak, and she plopped down on the stool. "Are you kids all alone? Please tell me someone else is there with you?"

"Just me and Aiden. I don't know where Emma is."

Shelley clapped a hand to her temple. "Emma's with Aunt Annie. She's keeping her until Uncle Dan picks her up on his way home." She looked up at the clock. "Hailey, are you guys okay?"

"Yeah, we're fine. And we had fun with Adelaide and Mr. Allan, but we weren't there long before Liddy came and brought us home."

Shelley looked out the window. The snow fell heavier than ever, small, businesslike flakes, but so thick she couldn't see the other side of the street. She didn't dare suggest that Hailey and Aiden go out into it, even to go back to Adelaide's or across the street to Diane's.

"Listen to me, honey. I'm going to come home as soon as I can. I've got a few customers, but I'll ask them to leave. And I have to turn off the machines and take care of the cash, but after that I'll come right home. Do you hear me?"

"Okay."

Hailey's voice sounded small.

Calm down, Shelley told herself. *You'll scare her.* She cleared her throat and tried to lighten her tone.

"So, what are you doing now?"

"We were watching a cartoon. Is that okay? Liddy put it on before she left. She said you or Uncle Dan would be home by the time it finished."

Shelley exhaled. That must be a full-length animated movie. She stifled her anger and tried to think what to do. "Look, I'm going to call Adelaide and Miss Diane. Maybe one of them can come over." Though she hated to ask Diane to do any more, knowing she was still recovering. "You hang in there, okay?"

"Okay."

"All right. I'll try to get home before that cartoon ends, and I'll call back if somebody else is coming over. Hailey, don't open the door to anyone but Uncle Dan or me, unless I call you back and tell you it's okay. You hear me?"

"I hear you."

Now she sounded terrified.

"Hey," Shelley said, softening her voice. "You're doing fine, Hailey. I'll be there soon."

"Okay."

Shelley hated to hang up, but she knew she couldn't help if she didn't.

"Good-bye, sweetie. Hang up the phone now and go back to watch TV with Aiden."

"Okay. Bye."

She waited until she heard the click and then disconnected her phone. When she went back to the counter, the newspaper-reading customer came up to the front with his mug.

"How about a refill?" he asked.

"Only if it's to go, I'm afraid," Shelley said. "I need to close up."

"Sure. Thanks."

She was relieved that no new customers had entered. She gave the man his coffee and then grabbed her cell phone.

She tried to call Margaret at the gallery, next door, but voice mail picked up, and then she tried the Hoskins' house phone. No one answered.

Diane, she thought. She really hated to ask Diane to go out in this horrible weather. She hesitated a moment, then called Diane's number, but got a busy signal.

She went out to the store and stood by the couple's table. "I'm sorry, folks, but I need to close and get out of here. Can I give you a refill to go?"

"No, we're good," the man said, rising.

Before they could get their coats on, the front door opened, and Bill the truck driver came in.

"Hey, Shelley. Can I get coffee?"

She wanted to blurt, "No, we're closed." Instead, she managed a smile. She had to empty the coffeepots anyway. "Sure, Bill, but you're the last. I'll go get it for you, but when these two go out the door, would you please turn the lock?" She flipped the Open sign to Closed herself, then strode back behind the counter.

She gave Bill a large coffee to go and two cookies and shooed him out the door, then dimmed the lights. She took a deep breath and ran over her mental list of chores. First would be cashing out—but not before she checked in with Hailey again.

This time Aiden answered the phone.

"Mommy!"

"Hey, buddy. Are you being good?"

"Yeah, but when are you coming home?"

"Soon," Shelley promised. "I have to close up the store, and then I'll come."

"The Cove store?"

"That's right."

"I want you here," Aiden whined.

"I know. I'll be there soon. Are you still watching your cartoon?"

"I got bored with it. I've seen it a bajillion times."

"Okay. Well, play with your trucks, then, but stay with Hailey and be good."

"Aunt Shelley?"

She heard a squawk from Aiden and assumed Hailey had wrestled the phone from him.

"Yes, Hailey?"

"It's dark outside."

"I know, honey. I'm going to get off so I can hurry and get there, okay? All my customers are gone, so it won't be long now."

"Okay. Bye."

Hailey hung up, and Shelley sprang into action. She would do the minimum cleanup, leaving anything that could wait until tomorrow morning. Certain things were mandatory for compliance with health regulations.

She was removing the used coffee grounds from one of the machines when her cell phone rang. The display showed "Dan," and she quickly opened the phone.

"Hey! Where are you?" she demanded. If Dan was home, she could take her time and stop worrying.

"We're in Augusta. Wayne's booked a room for us tonight."

"What!" Her own voice startled Shelley.

"Take it easy, Shell," Dan said. "The roads are treacherous. We're going to stay over. A lot of cars are going off the road, and Wayne doesn't want to take any chances."

"Okay," she said and gulped down her fear. "Honey, the babysitter left early."

"Huh?" Dan said.

"Liddy's father took her home early. Hailey and Aiden are alone at the house."

"Oh man! Hey, what about Emma? I'm supposed to pick her up."

"Can you call Annie?" Shelley said. "There's no way I can go get her tonight."

"Yeah, okay. I'll do that now."

"Thanks. I tried to call Allan, but nobody answered. And Margaret isn't next door at the gallery. I'm closing early, and I'm trying to get out of here and get home."

"You're still at the Cove?" Dan asked.

"Yes. Brenna cut herself, and I sent her to the hospital a couple of hours ago. In the rescue unit. I'm all alone here, Dan. I closed up, but I have a couple more things to do before I can leave."

He was silent for a moment. "Hailey's a smart kid. They'll be okay for a few minutes."

"I sure hope so."

When they had signed off, Shelley made herself clean the espresso machine and coffeemakers methodically. She put every dirty dish into the dishwasher and started it. Finally she hung up her apron and put on her boots, coat, hat, and mittens. She opened the back door. The snow still came down full force, blowing sideways in the wind. On the ground, it was nearly a foot deep in front of the door, and her white Outback was now covered in a thick white blanket.

She swallowed hard and waded out into the snow, thankful for her tall boots. Even so, the snow nearly reached the tops. As she surveyed the parking area, she began to doubt whether she could get her vehicle out. The town plow had scraped Main Street down nearly to the pavement again, but it had left a wicked-looking ridge of snow two feet high at the entrance to the Cove's small parking lot.

In a split second, she decided it would be better to walk home than to ram the small wagon into that snowbank with a good chance of getting it stuck there.

Just as this thought struck her, the cell phone in her pocket rang, displaying the Hoskins' number.

"Hello?"

"Shelley? It's Allan. You tried to call us?"

"Oh, Allan! Yes!" She let out a big sigh. "Thank you!"

"Are you okay? I was out in my shop, and Margaret and Adelaide were out with Elsa Kling and her girls, so when I came in the house, I saw that we'd missed a call. "

"It's the kids. The babysitter left them alone at my house. I've closed the Cove early, and I'm heading home, but I've got to walk, and—"

"You can't walk in this mess," Allan said. "I'll come and get you."

"But Aiden and Hailey—"

"It will only take me five minutes to come and get you. Are you ready to leave now?"

"Yes."

"All right, I'll be right there."

Allan hung up before she could protest.

Shelley walked back through the shop to the front door. She looked back to make sure she hadn't forgotten anything vital. At last she stepped outside.

A moment later a vehicle turned onto Main from Newport Avenue, and the headlights came toward her, illuminating the snow as it plummeted from the dark sky. Shelley stepped out into the street and flapped her arms. Allan stopped a few yards from her, letting the minivan slide to a halt as he rolled down his window.

"Hop in!"

Shelley didn't need any more urging to dive into the warm interior of the van.

"You should have waited inside," Allan said.

"I just stepped out. I figured it was as easy to meet you."

Allan drove on until he found a store lot that had been plowed recently enough to let him turn without fear of a mishap. He swung wide in a circle and headed back onto the street, pointed toward home.

Shelley related her misadventures to him on the way, and the problem with Liddy's abrupt departure.

"That's a shame," Allan said. "If we'd known, I could have gone right over to get them."

"I'm sure Dan will give her father a piece of his mind tomorrow," Shelley said.

"Well, the kids are probably doing fine. I'll go in with you to make sure."

The Bauers' driveway hadn't been plowed since morning. Dan usually did that with his pickup.

"You'd better not come in," Shelley said. "Looks like I have to wade."

"How high are your boots?" Allan asked.

"They're right up to my knees." Shelley opened her door, and the light came on, proving her point to him. Allan was wearing shoes. "I'll put the porch light on when I get inside so you'll know everything's okay," she said.

"All right, and if you don't do that immediately, I'm coming in."

"Deal. Thanks, Allan. I'm not sure I'd have made it without your help."

"You're welcome. Now, get going. I'm sitting right here until I see that porch light."

Shelley looked about for a place to cross the deep ridge of snow. Allan's headlights illuminated the yard. Her heart lurched when she glanced up and saw Aiden and Hailey watching her from the living room window. She waved and decided there was nothing to do but plunge in.

Her legs felt heavy as she slogged toward the door. This was worse than walking in knee-deep water. Snow had spilled over her boot tops and worked its way down her shins inside the leather. She pictured a tub full of scented hot water.

She turned the doorknob, but it didn't give. She pounded on the door with her mittened fists.

"Hailey! Open the door! It's me. Open up!"

The door opened inward so fast she nearly fell inside.

"Mama!" Aiden threw his arms around her thigh and squeezed.

She stooped and gathered him and Hailey into her arms. "Are you okay?"

"We're fine, Aunt Shelley," Hailey said.

"Oh, you good kids! I'm so proud of you!" Shelley squeezed them and straightened. "Quick now! We need to put on the porch light so Mr. Hoskins knows we're okay. Then he can go home."

Hailey rushed to the wall switch and flipped it. Shelley turned and stood in the doorway, waving at Allan for a moment, then firmly shut the door.

"I'm freezing! Let me get my boots off."

"I can make you some hot chocolate," Hailey said. "I can do it in the microwave, and I won't spill it."

"And I can get you some cookies," Aiden chimed in.

Shelley laughed. "I'll just bet you can. Maybe after we eat a real supper, okay?" She leaned against the doorjamb and toed off one boot.

The lights flickered and went out.

"Mommy!" Aiden shrieked.

"It's okay."

They both plowed back into her embrace. She held them close.

"It's really okay. We've got a flashlight in the kitchen drawer, remember? And another one in my bedroom. But I am *so* glad that I got here before this happened."

CHAPTER SEVENTEEN

In the morning, Beverly awoke to the sound of a plow truck passing the house. She rose and went to the window. The driveway was level with snow again, probably at least eighteen inches deep where it hadn't drifted. Add the bank that the plow had left across the edge of the street, and she knew she couldn't get out until the driveway was plowed. At least she didn't have to worry about town business today—the municipal office would be closed all day Saturday.

She got dressed and tiptoed down the stairs. The puppy whimpered in his cage. She dreaded taking him out, but there was no way around it. She put on her coat, high boots, and all the other accessories that went with winter, and opened the door of the dog crate.

The pup made a beeline for the door before she could catch him. She sighed and followed, clipping on his leash before opening the front door.

Snow had drifted up on the porch, and it grew progressively deeper from the door to the top of the steps, until she was standing in four inches as she contemplated the wisdom of going down into the yard. The puppy lifted his feet alternately and whined.

Beverly sighed. If the little dog stepped off the edge of the porch, he would flounder in the deep snow. She might have to resort to newspapers this morning—outside on the porch, of course. She looped the end of the leash around one of the porch balusters and went in to get an old paper from the recycling box.

When she came back out, the little dog was huddled against the newel post, shivering. A foot away was his morning contribution.

Beverly couldn't help but laugh. She crouched down and patted him.

"Good boy. You couldn't wait, could you?"

He whimpered and then gave one little bark.

"Yeah, I hear you. That stuff is cold." Beverly picked him up. "Come on. You can go in while I get rid of it." She had left the little scooper she took on their walks on the porch, leaning against the outside wall of the house.

When she went inside, he was lying on the hall rug. He looked up at her plaintively.

Beverly chuckled. "It's okay, little guy. Are you hungry now?"

His tail began to wag. She hung up her coat and put away her boots, hat, and gloves. Pulling on the slippers she kept in the hall closet, she continued to talk to him. "Yeah, I'll feed you. I still don't like dogs, but I wouldn't let you starve. Come on, mutt."

She headed for the kitchen, and the puppy jumped up and tagged along.

The house phone rang, and she glanced at the clock in surprise. It was barely seven o'clock. She grabbed the receiver before it could ring again.

"Hello?" she said cautiously.

"Mayor Wheeland?" a man's voice said.

"Yes."

"Do you know when the plow is going to do Hill Road again? I have to go to Willow Corners today, and I can't get out."

"Uh, no, I don't. I'm sorry." She thought back to when she'd awakened half an hour ago. The plow was doing the side streets in town then. It might take a while for them to get to the outlying roads. "Was your road plowed in the night?"

"I heard them go by once—maybe midnight or so. But there's about six or eight inches of new snow out there now."

"I can try to call the road commissioner and get an estimate for you." Beverly reached for a notepad. "Would you please give me your name and number? I'll get back to you."

She took down the man's information and hung up the phone. She really didn't want to call the road commissioner this early. He'd probably been up half the night. For all she knew, he might even be out in the plow that was clearing the town's streets right now.

The puppy whined. He was sitting on the linoleum at her feet, looking up at her, his head cocked to one side.

"Sorry. I forgot about you, didn't I?"

Beverly decided to feed the pup and make a pot of coffee before she called the road commissioner. A few minutes later she decided that might have been a mistake. The phone rang again as she was measuring out the ground coffee.

"Hello, Wheeland residence," she said into the phone.

"Is this the mayor?"

"Yes."

The caller was a woman this time. "I live on Ranken Road, and the snowplow took out my mailbox sometime during the night."

Beverly put a hand to her forehead. "I'm sorry to hear that. If you'll give me your name and phone number, I'll discuss it with the road commissioner."

Something told her this was going to be a long day.

* * *

Shelley was up early and baking when Dan got home. She saw his pickup come down Newport Avenue and stop out front, where the driveway ended. He waded through the snow carrying his lunchbox, and she met him at the door.

"Hey! Thanks for coming early." She put her arms around him.

He bent to kiss her. "Was it too awful?"

"No, but the kids are still asleep. They were pretty worn out from the anxiety, I think. But Hailey did great. Aiden too. I was so proud of them."

"What about Emma?"

"Annie called me after you talked to her last night. She says to call her when our driveway's cleared and she'll bring her home."

"Good," Dan said.

"Yeah, I guess she was kind of fussy last night. Poor little thing."

They had walked into the kitchen as they talked, and Dan set his lunchbox on the table. "Aren't you supposed to open the Cove about now?"

"I'm going to open a few minutes late. So sue me."

Dan laughed. "How's Brenna?"

"As of about ten last night, she was doing okay. I told her to take today off, but she says she'll come in later if she feels all right. Parker will come in today and help me."

"Sounds like you've got everything under control, boss woman."

Shelley winced. "I'm not sure I like the sound of that. But at least you're here now, so I can leave. I'd better get suited up."

"I'll shovel you a path while you get ready," Dan said.

"That would be great." Shelley hugged him again. "I am *so* glad you're home."

"Daddy!"

She stepped back as Aiden dashed into the kitchen and catapulted into Dan's arms.

★ ★ ★

Diane walked slowly along the sidewalk with Rocky on his leash. The sun glittered on the new snow. Everywhere people were out blowing it from their driveways or shoveling their walks. She waved to those who looked her way. Rocky hadn't been downtown for some time, and he seemed to find the new sights and smells fascinating. He paused often to sniff the snowbanks and strained at the leash when he saw something interesting ahead.

"Let's go as far as Old First, boy," Diane said to the eager dog. "I haven't walked that far for quite a while."

She still felt able to go on, and that pleased her. She wanted to get stronger. Winter would not hold her back.

As they approached the old stone church, she saw a figure moving rapidly about the parking lot. Curious, she urged Rocky along. When they got closer, he barked and pulled her forward, toward the jogger who was taking advantage of the cleared but empty parking lot. At an answering yip, Diane jerked her head to the side and smiled. Beverly's little gray puppy was hitched to a lamppost beside the walk to the imposing front entrance of the church.

Beverly caught sight of her and jogged over, slowing as she approached.

"Hello! You're quite a ways from home this morning."

"I could say the same about you," Diane said.

"I haven't been able to jog for the last two days," Beverly said. "I thought we'd do a longer walk this morning. When I saw this open space, I realized it was perfect. I'm not sure the puppy appreciates it, though. He's probably restless."

Diane moved slowly toward the puppy, who jumped and pulled at his leash. "Rocky wants to say hello."

"I'd better untie him." Beverly walked over and removed the leash from the lamppost. She let the puppy have enough slack so that he and Rocky could touch noses.

"They like meeting a friend on their walks as much as we do," Diane said.

"Looks like it."

"How's it going with him?"

Beverly's expression clouded. "I hate to admit it, but not very well. In fact, Jeff and I had a fight about it."

Diane stared at her. "I'm so sorry."

Beverly sighed. "He called at a bad time, and I sort of let loose on him. It was a big mistake on my part, but I'm not sure what to do about it. He offered to find someone who would take the puppy, and I said no."

"Maybe that would be for the best," Diane said softly. She'd had hopes for Beverly in this new venture, but she certainly didn't want to see her friend more stressed and fighting with her fiancé.

Beverly gazed down at the fluffy gray pup. "I'm getting used to having him around, but I'm not sure I want to."

"This spring you'll be able to take him with you when you jog on the beach."

"Yes, I'm looking forward to it. That's going to be another month or two, I'm afraid."

Diane looked around at the huge snowbanks the plow had left along the perimeter of Old First's parking lot. "It's pretty, but I hope this was our last big storm of the year."

"*I* hope it's our last plowable storm."

"Oh?" Diane eyed her keenly. "Something I don't know?"

Beverly shrugged. "It's just that I've had several complaints today about the plowing, or lack of it."

"I thought they did a good job."

"Well, you live right in town. The folks on the back roads aren't happy, and I'm afraid a couple of people lost their mailboxes. I spoke to Jules Benton about that, and he tells me the town has made it a past policy not to pay for damage to mailboxes. He says usually when that happens, the box was too close to the pavement, but I don't know."

"I suppose it would set a precedent, and you'd get a ton of claims," Diane said.

"I'm going to look into it, but in the meantime I'm going to refer any new callers to him or the road commissioner."

"Good. You don't need the added stress." Diane looked toward the street. "I guess we should head back now."

"We'll come with you," Beverly said. "Maybe you can give me some more ideas on how to get this mutt to stop chewing everything in sight."

Diane chuckled. "*Shh.* He's in a much higher social class than a mutt! But seriously, he's going to chew until all his teeth are in. The best I can tell you is provide him with lots of chew toys and rawhide strips. And keep everything else up out of reach."

"I got that message loud and clear," Beverly said. "I actually think the puppy has made some progress—but he keeps finding new things to chew. Things I wouldn't have expected. The other day, he was gnawing on a paperback book. Can you imagine?"

"Maybe he has a literary turn," Diane said drily.

"Right." Beverly huffed out a cloud of vapor. "Sounds like I need to make another trip to the pet store."

"The more chew toys you give him, the less likely that he'll get bored with those. Try to find different textures for him."

"That makes sense." Beverly gave her a wry smile. "I don't know as I've ever received a gift before that turned out to be this expensive."

"It sounds as though you plan to keep him." Diane watched her closely.

"Oh, I'm keeping him. But I've got to find ways to enjoy him, instead of resenting him. I don't like the tension with Jeff one little bit."

★ ★ ★

"Those are perfect!" Nicole picked up one of the radish roses Margaret had made. "I couldn't have done it better myself."

Margaret smiled. Finally, she was starting to feel more confident about food preparation. "And I can make them early in the day?"

"Yes, if you put them in water in the refrigerator until the last minute. But don't cut any of the other salad vegetables more than twenty minutes ahead."

"Got it. I think cutting fancy vegetables is easier for me than actually cooking something."

"Of course—it's your artistic eye. But your salad dressing came out well too." Nicole opened the refrigerator and took out a plastic container. "Take this with you to use for your dinner. It will last just fine in the fridge."

"Thanks."

"Next time we'll do appetizers again, and a trial run of the entrée."

"I can't thank you enough." Margaret reached for her jacket.

Nicole shrugged. "Doing this in exchange for my art lessons is great, but seeing you smile when something comes out right—that's worth a million bucks."

Margaret chuckled. "I know what you mean. That's how I felt the first time you were satisfied with the way the sky looked on your canvas."

She hurried to her car, realizing she was running a little later than she liked. When she drove past the gallery, it was dark. She hadn't opened today, using the heavy snowfall for an excuse. That morning, she'd told Allan she wanted to go shopping—and she had, but she'd kept that short and sweet and then dashed to Nicole's house for her cooking session.

The Cove, as usual, was open, and she wondered how Shelley was doing. The poor girl must be exhausted after this trying week.

She turned onto Newport Avenue with a sense of relief. She was home. Adelaide met her at the door, eyes aglitter.

"What did you make today, Mom?"

"*Shh.*" Margaret looked past her toward the kitchen door. "Where's Dad?"

"He's making supper. What did you cook?"

"Honey, you can't talk about it, remember?" Margaret whispered. "He might hear you, and it's a surprise."

Adelaide nodded eagerly. "But what did you—"

"Appetizers and salad, but that's just between you and me."

"Okay."

Margaret eyed her closely. "You didn't tell him, did you?"

Adelaide shook her head. "He said you went shopping."

"I did." Margaret handed her a plastic store bag. "I got you some new socks and the notebook you need for school."

Eagerly, Adelaide opened the bag. "Oh! It has a kitty on it."

"I hope that's all right." Margaret wondered if she should have gotten a plain notebook with a solid-colored cover, but Adelaide's delight told her that she had chosen right.

"I love it."

Allan appeared in the kitchen doorway. "Hi. Everything all right?"

"Dad, look what Mom brought me!" Adelaide hurried over to show him the notebook.

"I like that," Allan said with a smile. He darted Margaret a glance. "Supper in about ten minutes."

"I'll be ready." Now, how would she slip the container of salad dressing into the refrigerator without Allan becoming suspicious? She considered writing "Adelaide" on the lid.

Maybe he would think it was something their daughter was going to take to school. But Allan handled all the food in the house, so he would probably ask Adelaide about it, and that could lead to disaster. Better to sneak it to Beverly's or Diane's if she could.

For the time being, she stashed the bag with the container in her closet. This life of intrigue certainly was stressful.

★ ★ ★

Shelley turned the lock on the Cove's front door for the last time. Since Saturday was her final day at the store, she'd stayed late to lock up, cash out, and make sure everything was shipshape for Rusty. Parker had helped all morning, and Brenna, who had a bandage on her left hand, had come in at noon. Brenna couldn't handle the customers' food today, but she had insisted she'd be as efficient as ever at the cash register, so Shelley had let her work.

"I'll sweep the flow-uh if you can do the wiping up," Brenna called to her.

"Sure thing." Shelley set to work on the cleanup chores, letting Brenna do the tasks that didn't involve water. By six thirty they were ready to leave. Shelley took a last look around and exhaled deeply.

"Tired?" Brenna asked.

"Yeah, but it feels good. We did a good job this week."

Brenna smiled. "We had a few crazy moments, but yeah. *You* did a terrific job. Are you coming in Monday to see Rusty?"

"Oh yeah. I'll be here around six with fresh pastries."

"That reminds me, you may as well take home the leftovers tonight. We can't leave them over Sunday."

"You take them," Shelley said. "There're only a couple of cookies and a few muffins."

"You sure?"

"I'm sure. My family gets all my rejects."

"Thanks." Brenna picked up the box of leftover baked goods. "It was lots of fun working with you, Shelley. I hope you do take over for Rusty."

"We'll see. There are some things I'd have to work out, that's for sure."

"Your kids?" Brenna asked.

"That's the biggest one."

"I hope you figure it out." Brenna laughed. "It'd be awful to have to break in a new boss."

Shelley gave her a hug. "You've been great this week, even when things got tough. Now, let's go home."

CHAPTER EIGHTEEN

Shelley scrambled to get out of the house before six on Monday morning so she could get her wares to the Cove, talk to Rusty for a few minutes, and get home before Dan left to meet his boss.

Rusty let her in the back door, grinning from ear to ear. "Hey there! Everything looks great."

"Thanks." Shelley set several containers of pastries down on the worktable.

"Sorry you had to get the repairman in here."

"Yeah, it might be time to think about getting a new espresso machine."

He scowled at that.

Shelley took off her gloves and opened the container of muffins. "I'll put these in the case for you." She took a pair of disposable gloves from the box on the table.

Rusty cocked his head toward his left shoulder and gazed at her. "So tell me."

"Tell you what?"

"Have you decided?"

Shelley sighed and carried the muffin box to the display case at the counter. Rusty followed her and watched her arrange the goodies on the shelves.

"Rusty, if I were going to do something like this..."

"Yeah?"

"Let me just say that I've never in my life been so relieved as I was yesterday, when you phoned and told me you and Wendy were home."

"Oh."

She turned to face him. "It was really hard. I'm not afraid of hard work, but with all the stuff going on here and child care problems at home, I don't know."

Rusty's face fell. "I guess you'd have to work out something for the kids."

"That was the worst part of it for me. It put quite a strain on us. But I also realized it really would take away from my baking time. And you know what? I was tired all the time."

"That's part of the territory," Rusty said. "I've been tired for thirty years."

Shelley shook her head. "I'm glad you got your vacation, but I'm not sure I could do that."

"But you're still thinking about it, right?" Hope gleamed in Rusty's warm blue eyes. "You know, Brenna could handle most of the coffee operation for you, so you could bake more. And you can train other people. I get a couple of high school kids in here every week, asking if I'm hiring. If you wanted to expand the bakery business, you could, and still keep the coffee counter open."

Shelley sighed. She should just say no, right now, end of story. "Dan and I haven't hashed it out completely," she admitted. Over the weekend they had talked as if Rusty's return was the end of Shelley's commitment to the Cove, but they hadn't exactly spelled that out.

"So when can you let me know?"

"Soon. But don't get your hopes up."

She went back to the worktable for the container of Danish. The idea of having her own storefront bakery still tempted her. She could picture where she would put in extra glass-fronted cases for her baked goods. She could sell a lot of retail right here at the Cove, once the word got out.

The back door flew open, and Brenna came in stamping snow off her boots.

"Good morning, Shelley! Hi, Rusty, how was your trip?"

Shelley greeted Brenna and puttered about, stocking the displays. She would miss Brenna's cheerful chatter, greeting the early coffee regulars, and meeting new customers daily. But she wouldn't miss the headaches, not one bit.

She peeled off her disposable gloves and stacked her empty containers. "I'll see you all later!" She headed out the back door and home to her family.

* * *

Diane got into Beverly's car on Monday and buckled her seat belt. "You know, I feel almost normal today. It's too bad I can't just carry on as if I were."

"You need to finish the course of treatment." Beverly set the car in motion, heading for the cancer center in Augusta.

"I know, but it doesn't seem fair." Diane chuckled. "Don't listen to me. I know life's not fair. I'm going to stick this out and be healthy again."

"That's better."

"Thanks so much for doing this. Every time we go, I think I could drive myself. But when it's time to leave the clinic, I am *so* glad I'm not driving."

Beverly smiled at her. "I'm happy to do it. It makes me slow down for a few hours and remember to enjoy my friends."

"Do you mind if I quote you on my blog? Because that might be a help to some people. Stop thinking of it as a trip to the icky place, and look at it as some quiet time with the person who's with you."

"Sure, but don't feel as though you have to talk to me all morning. I know for some people at least, those icky feelings are pretty severe during treatments, and afterward too."

"That's one of the hardest times—afterward. I hope I can help people, even just a teeny bit. Having you and Shelley and Margaret close by is such a blessing. Lots of patients don't get the support I do." Diane leaned back and closed her eyes for a moment. "You know, Leo called me again last night."

"Oh?"

One thing Diane loved about Beverly was that she didn't pry. She was more than willing to listen if another person wanted to share something personal, but she would never probe for details. Instead, she waited for her friend to feel comfortable laying the situation out there.

"He offered to drive me today." Diane looked over at Beverly.

"That was nice of him."

"Yes. He would have canceled his appointments this morning to stay with me. I thanked him and said I knew his patients needed him. I'd have felt guilty if I'd kept him away from his practice today. All those animals needing care! He can't put them off for hours. But he's so sweet and thoughtful toward me."

"He is." Beverly merged on to the road that would take them to Augusta.

"I told him maybe soon I'd enjoy an evening game of Scrabble with him."

"That sounds like fun."

Diane sighed and laid her head back again. "I think so. I told him I'd call by the end of the week, if I feel all right."

"And if you don't, he'll probably call again to make sure you're okay."

Diane nodded. "He made me promise to tell him if I was too tired, but I know he'd like that. The Scrabble game, I mean. We left it that I'll call when I'm ready."

The routine at the clinic went much as usual. Diane hadn't experienced many side effects from this course, other than the ongoing fatigue between treatments. Once she was settled in, with her IV in place, she brought up the subject of dogs.

"How's the puppy doing?"

"A little better, I think," Beverly said. "I did get him some more toys, and since he'd ruined a pair of slippers, we designated those as the puppy's and bought new ones for my father."

"How about Jeff?" Diane asked softly.

"I e-mailed him last night. I tried to call once and didn't get him, so I sent a short note, just saying don't worry about the puppy, it's fine."

"I hope it works out." Now might be a good time to redirect the conversation. Diane smiled. "So, any progress on the train station mystery?"

"I haven't gotten to the newspaper archives," Beverly said. "I need to get in there when I've got a chunk of time and can dig up and comb through the 1951 and 1952 papers and look for anything about the railroad."

Diane nodded. "The four of us need to get together again too. Now that Shelley's finished at the Cove, maybe we can do that."

"Let's try by the end of the week."

"That sounds good." Diane looked around for the nurse who'd been checking on her regularly. "I'm a little thirsty. Do you see the nurse?"

Beverly jumped up. "Let me get you something. Would you like juice, tea, water? They have a pretty good stock of beverages."

"Juice, I think. Thanks." Diane leaned back and closed her eyes. She sent up a prayer for strength, knowing the medicine flowing into her body was designed to help her.

Beverly came back with two Styrofoam cups. "I've got orange juice and grape. Which would you like?"

"Grape, thanks." Diane took the cup she offered and sipped it. The cold, sweet liquid immediately perked her up. "That hits the spot. I think my sugar must have been a little low."

Beverly sat down and sipped her orange juice. After a moment she asked, "Are you doing okay now?"

"Yes, I'm fine."

"You know, I sort of forgot about contacting the caretaker for the Thorpe house. The Inglewood house, I mean. I should have tried to call him again, but it slipped my mind."

"Do you have his number in your cell?" Diane asked.

"I do."

Diane arched her eyebrows. "Well? Nothing could liven up a treatment session more than searching for clues."

Beverly chuckled. "Okay. If you're sure." She glanced around at the room full of people. Everyone seemed immersed in their own conversations with their companions or the medical staff.

Beverly took her phone from her purse. "Willard Rockwell. Okay, here goes!" She pushed a few keys and waited. "Hello, Mr. Rockwell? This is Beverly Wheeland. Yes, the mayor. Oh, thank you."

Diane smiled as she watched her friend. Beverly had become the efficient public servant. If anyone could get the information they sought, she could.

Beverly explained to the caretaker why she had called. She listened for a moment and then said, "I see. Do you have a way to contact them before May?"

Diane could see that the call wasn't producing the fruit they'd hoped for, but Beverly was thinking ahead. Mr. Rockwell must have a way to reach the Inglewoods if some catastrophe occurred at their home. She took another sip of her grape juice and waited.

A moment later, Beverly hung up, her mouth scrunched in disappointment.

"No go?" Diane asked.

"No, he said he doesn't know much about the house's history. He didn't even recognize Elias Thorpe's name. And he said he's not supposed to give out the Inglewoods' contact information. They travel a lot in winter, and they don't want to be disturbed unless something big happens. We have to respect that."

Diane sighed. "Of course you're right, and our inquiry is hardly an emergency."

"Agreed," Beverly said. "We don't want to bother them. Guess we'll just have to wait until the snowbirds fly back home."

When the treatment ended, Diane declined a wheelchair and walked out to the car with Beverly.

"How are you doing?" Beverly asked, holding the passenger door for her.

"Not too bad." Diane slid into the car and buckled up while Beverly went around and got in behind the wheel.

"Straight home? If you have any errands, I'm good to do some running for you."

"I can't think of anything." Diane relaxed, and soon she was back in her cheerful little cottage.

Beverly saw her inside and urged her to call if she needed help with anything.

"I actually feel better than I did the last time," Diane said. "I may even work on my blog this afternoon."

"Well, at least let me take Rocky out for a quick walk."

"You don't have to do that," Diane said.

Beverly laughed. "I don't mind. I'm getting to be quite the expert dog walker."

A few minutes later, Diane and Rocky were alone. Instead of sitting down at her computer, Diane sank onto the sofa. Rocky came over and sat next to her, gazing into her face.

"I'm okay, boy." She patted his smooth golden head. "I just thought I might sit here and read for a little while."

Rocky lay down on the rug beside her, and Diane settled back into the cushions. The fatigue she had evaded earlier found her, and she didn't bother to reach for a book. Instead, she let herself drift into sleep.

Her ringing phone woke her some time later, and she shifted on the cushions to take it from her pocket.

"Hello?" She felt a little befuddled.

"Mom?"

"Jessica." Diane smiled and sat up. "Hi, honey."

"Today's your treatment, isn't it?"

"All done and back home again."

"How did that go?"

"Pretty well. Beverly drove me again and she stayed with me, though she didn't have to. I told her I'd be fine if she wanted to go shopping for a while, but she stuck it out. We had a good time together, if you can believe that."

Jessica laughed. "Trust you to make a cancer treatment into a social event, Mom."

"How are things going with Martin?" Diane asked.

"Much better. He's looking into taking a couple of education classes at BU this summer."

"Oh, that's terrific!"

"Yeah, he's starting to get excited about it. His boss said he can go part-time in his IT work at the end of April. Martin seems a lot happier these days."

"I'm so glad you worked that out."

"Me too. Mom, he thought I'd get all bent out of shape if he left his job. Can you imagine?"

"He knows you better now, and how strong and supportive you are."

"I don't know about that," Jessica said.

"I do. You've been a rock for me, all through this illness, even though you aren't close by. Martin should have known you'd back him up. He's seen you be there for me. And remember that time you brought him to meet me, and I was having a sugar low?"

"Yeah. You wound up in the hospital."

"And you were wonderful. You'll do the same for Martin. Honey, as he gets to know you better, he'll understand that about you."

"Thanks, Mom. I'm seeing new sides of his personality too. I think he's going to make a great teacher."

Jessica sounded a little teary, so Diane decided to switch to a more upbeat topic.

"Of course he will. Hey, did I tell you that Beverly has a new puppy?"

"What? No. I didn't know she liked dogs."

Diane laughed. "She doesn't. Jeff gave it to her as a surprise. He's a sweet little schnoodle. And you know what? I think the little ball of gray fluff is growing on her."

Diane eased back on the pillows and chatted happily for fifteen minutes. Finally, Jessica said, "Well, my lunch hour's up. Did you eat yet?"

"No, not yet," Diane said.

"You'd better go do it right now," Jessica said sternly. "No more sugar lows for you."

"Okay, I will."

Jessica sighed. "Great talking to you, Mom. Love you."

Savoring those sweet words, Diane signed off and put the phone away. She stood up, and Rocky, anticipating some activity, stood too.

"Come on," Diane said. "Time for one of us to eat, and then maybe we'll stroll over to Shelley's and see how she likes being at home all day."

* * *

Guilt nagged at Margaret as she drove to Nicole's house Monday afternoon. She hadn't lied to Allan about her destination, but she had let him think she was headed to her usual tai chi class at the community center.

Today they were preparing her special chicken dish. If she could make this come out right and fine-tune the timing on the other dishes, she might be able to pull off her surprise.

Everything seemed to turn out so well when she had Nicole at her side coaching her. But could she really make it work when she was alone?

After the lesson, she picked up Adelaide at the community center.

"Did you have fun today?" Margaret asked as her daughter got into the car.

"Uh-huh. I played games with the middle grade kids and worked on crafts with them."

"Do you have homework for tomorrow's classes?"

Adelaide shook her head. "I got everything done over the weekend."

Margaret tried to make sure Adelaide went to her community college child development classes well prepared, but lately she'd been so busy with the cooking, tai chi, the gallery, and her own painting, that she had let Allan do more of the supervising.

"Well, I'll have you know that my cooking turned out perfect today. I brought you a taste of the appetizers." She handed Adelaide a small container.

"Oh boy! You didn't burn them."

"No, not this time. I decided to go with something that's not as delicate as the crab puffs. These won't be spoiled if I don't get the timing exactly right."

Adelaide ate one of the spinach and pesto pinwheels. "It tastes weird."

Margaret smiled. "Weird how? Icky weird or just different weird?"

"Different. I think it's good."

"That's a relief. I liked it myself. And I'm going to do little meatballs too. They're a lot easier than the puff pastry. And you only eat a little of the appetizers, because you have to save room for the rest of the meal."

"Dad will like it." Adelaide nodded firmly, as though that settled everything.

"I sure hope he does," Margaret said. "Now, I'm planning to do this on Wednesday. Did you remember to talk to your friends about dinner that night?"

"Uh-huh. I'm going to eat with Mrs. Kling and Maryann."

"You don't mind, do you?"

Adelaide shook her head. "They're fun."

"Yes, they are." Margaret smiled. "I hope you help me decorate before you go. You're really good with flowers and things like that."

"Sure, Mom."

"Great. But we still can't tell Dad."

"How will he not know?" Adelaide seemed truly puzzled.

"I'm going to send him on an errand that will take a while. And if he won't go, I may have to tell him we're fixing a surprise for him. I don't want to do that, but it will be a last resort."

Adelaide nodded, content with that. Margaret hoped that this time, she could make the evening turn out the way she intended.

CHAPTER NINETEEN

A crash awakened Beverly, and she sat bolt upright in bed. Rain was beating against her bedroom windows. A moment later, flickering lightning illuminated everything in rapid, strobelike flashes. Another peal of thunder boomed, seemingly right over the roof of the house.

She exhaled deeply and eased back down on her pillow. This was freakish weather for February. Normally, they got several good, stiff snowstorms this time of year. But occasionally, if a warm front came through, they got rain. She hoped it would compact the snow and make it easy to keep the road clear for a while.

Going back to sleep would be best, if she could do it with the noises of the storm enveloping the house. Lying awake and fretting would be useless. Her alarm clock still glowed, so the power was on. She had a flashlight at hand if she needed it, and her computer was plugged into a surge protector. She inhaled gradually and willed her pulse to slow.

Between the thunder's rumblings, an intermittent whine reached her. She frowned and threw back the bedclothes. A sharp yip, muffled by the distance between them, reached her right before another bolt of lightning flashed, followed almost at once by thunder so loud a freight train might have been rolling through the house.

Beverly turned on the bedside lamp and poked her feet into her slippers. She strode to the door and opened it. Sure enough, the puppy was crying. Not barking, crying. He sounded in Beverly's ears like a terrified child.

Unable to ignore the sound, she tiptoed down the stairs, though she doubted her father was still asleep. In the kitchen, she turned on the overhead light. The puppy sat quivering in his kennel, gazing out at her. He whined again, almost like a sob.

"Are you scared?" Beverly crouched down and opened the door of the kennel so she could stroke his head. He leaned into her hand, and she let her fingers slide along his spine. "It's just thunder. It'll go away."

Another *boom* made her jump, and when she recovered, her heart was pounding and she had a writhing gray puppy in her arms. He shoved his nose beneath her arm and trembled.

"Well! I guess you *are* scared." She stood and carried him up the stairs. She felt a little silly as she settled on the bed with the pup. He curled up on the quilt next to her, with his chin resting on her arm.

Beverly reached over and patted his head. "It's okay."

The rain pelted the windows, and the lightning flashes continued. A particularly loud crash of thunder sent the puppy up onto her chest.

"Hey!" Beverly sat up and arranged the extra pillow behind her so that she was half sitting and could hold the puppy on her lap, on top of the covers. She was about to turn off the lamp when her father appeared in her doorway, knocking on the open door.

"Hi. I thought I heard you get up, and then I saw your light. Is everything—" His jaw dropped as he spotted the puppy on her lap. He stepped forward, staring. "Well, well. What do you know?"

"He was whining down there." Beverly's cheeks warmed. "Between him and the thunder, I couldn't sleep. Besides, he was scared."

"Poor little guy." Her father leaned down and scratched the puppy's head between his ears. "Hey, fella. It's lots nicer up here, isn't it?"

"I hope I haven't given him ideas about coming upstairs." Beverly wasn't sure she'd have brought him up if she'd thought of that earlier. "I thought the power might go out, though. Then he'd be really scared."

Her father nodded. "The lights on the stove and the microwave are little nightlights for him. I wouldn't like it either if it went completely dark." He yawned and clapped a hand over his mouth to stifle it. "Well, I'd better shuffle off."

"Do you want to take him?" she asked, hoping he'd agree. She would certainly stay awake if she kept the puppy in her room.

"I think you're doing just fine," her father said, a bit too amused for her liking.

As he reached the doorway, Beverly called, "You won't tell Mrs. Peabody, will you?"

"Who, me?" He smiled at her. "Good night."

* * *

Margaret tried to come up with a way to keep Allan from suspecting her plans, but no flash of inspiration helped her. "Would you be able to tend the gallery tomorrow afternoon?" she asked him over breakfast on Tuesday.

"I usually do on Wednesday." He sipped his coffee placidly.

"I meant *all* afternoon," Margaret said.

"I suppose so." He cocked his head to one side and studied her. "You've been up to something lately."

"You're not supposed to know," Adelaide said, frowning at him.

"Adelaide, do you have your books in your backpack?" Margaret asked hastily.

Adelaide blinked at her. "Uh-huh."

"And did you feed the cats?"

Adelaide nodded.

Margaret racked her brain for another reason to get her daughter away from the table.

"She has plenty of time," Allan said. "She doesn't have to meet the bus for another half hour."

Margaret picked up half an English muffin and took a bite. He knew, that was all. He knew. Adelaide had probably blabbed the whole thing to him yesterday.

"So what time do you need me tomorrow?" Allan asked.

"One o'clock?" Margaret asked.

"Sure. I guess you have errands to run before tai chi?"

"Yes." *Errands right here in our kitchen,* Margaret thought. And she'd stashed the extra food in Diane's refrigerator this time. Fetching that could be considered an errand.

"I'll make sure the gas tank is filled." Allan got up and went to the counter to refill his coffee mug.

Margaret watched him, trying to discern some clue in his actions that would tell her how much he knew.

"Mom doesn't need to go to the store again," Adelaide said.

"How do you know?" Margaret asked quickly.

Adelaide stared at her for a moment and then raised one hand to cover her mouth. Margaret nodded but then winked at her. She didn't want Adelaide to think she was angry with her.

"Come on." Margaret pushed her chair back and picked up her dirty dishes. "I'll take you to the bus stop this morning before I go to the gallery. You'll need your umbrella today."

"She'll be too early," Allan said. "Margaret, what is going on?"

Setting the dishes on the counter, she huffed out a big breath and allowed her shoulders to slump. "Nothing bad, okay? Just...cooperate."

A smile slowly crept over Allan's face. "All right, I guess I can do that. You get along to the gallery, though. I'll take Adelaide to the bus stop as usual. And I won't pump her for information, if that's what you're afraid of."

"I won't tell him, Mom," Adelaide said, looking anxiously back and forth between them.

"I know you won't, honey." Margaret walked over and drew her into a hug. "And if you did, the world wouldn't end. But let's try to keep it between us for one more day, okay?"

Adelaide nodded eagerly.

Margaret kissed her cheek. "I'll see you later." She threw Allan a mock glare. "You too."

★ ★ ★

When Beverly drove to the *Courier* office, the rain had slacked to a drizzle. The snowbanks in all the parking lots had shrunk measurably, and Main Street's pavement was bare. The newspaper's lot held a sloppy mess of slush and water. She chose her parking spot carefully, to be sure she could get out without wading.

Abby Lane, who handled most of the paper's advertising, looked up as Beverly entered. Her desk was positioned near the door, and she also answered most calls to the paper.

"Hi, Abby," Beverly said.

"Good morning, Mayor. Can I help you?"

"I'd like to go up to your archives. You still have copies of the 1950s *Couriers*, don't you?"

"Yes, most of them, in bound volumes—the ones that escaped the fire fifty years ago. Do you need help? You've been up there before, haven't you?"

"Yes, I have been. I should be all right."

Abby nodded. "I go up there as seldom as possible myself."

"Can't say I blame you, but thanks." Beverly walked through the main room and past several smaller offices to the stairway. The steps were narrow and lit by one rather dim bulb high overhead. The building had at one time housed a corset factory, and one of its oddities was that the stairs on the next level were at the opposite end of the structure. To reach them, she had to wend her way through a maze of old sewing machines and other equipment on the second story.

Finally she reached the next flight of stairs and climbed them, trying not to think about spiders and dirt. No railing helped her climb to the third level. When she emerged in the long, narrow attic, she wrinkled her nose at the dusty, neglected scent.

In the low-ceilinged room, metal shelves lined the walls on both sides. The big bound volumes of old newspapers were stacked on them, and Beverly knew from past experience that they were not stored in chronological order. She squinted at the spines of the huge books in the nearest shelf unit. The first ones were from 1913 and 1914, but on a higher shelf she found several months from 1952 that she and Diane had missed on their previous visit. She hauled them out and laid them on the dust-coated oak table in the middle of the dimly lit room.

She kept hunting until she'd found all of 1951 and most of 1952. With the big books laid out on the table, she began with January 1951. Leafing through the yellowed pages, she tried not to allow herself to be distracted by the ads and society columns, but looked instead for business stories, especially items having to do with the railroad or the quarry.

A quick scan of a society page in the March volume slowed her down, however. Below a wedding announcement was an account of a lavish party, hosted by none other than Elias Thorpe. In the fall, she and Diane had found a similar article which described the bash the stationmaster had thrown when the president of the railroad visited in December 1951. Apparently, Elias Thorpe was the cream of Marble Cove society in the fifties—or at least had wanted to be.

She read with interest the account, which included the guest list. She recognized a few surnames from Marble Cove families, but some of the guests seemed to be from out of town. The menu made her mouth water. Onion soup au gratin, steamship round of beef, fried shrimp, chicken rosemary, baked sea bass, sweet potatoes, red potato salad, green beans jardinière, orange rolls, and assorted pickles and preserves. That was all before dessert. *Quite a spread for early spring in those days*, Beverly thought. The article listed three desserts: Lady Baltimore cake, chocolate raspberry torte, and lemon ice. Her stomach rumbled.

Beverly took out her phone and snapped a couple of pictures of the article. She wasn't sure how well they would turn out with the poor lighting in the attic, so she took a notebook from her purse and jotted down some details from the account, including the guests' names. The fact that the bound volumes were large and awkward, and the paper crumbled if she wasn't careful, frustrated her mightily. She longed to take photocopies of articles to her friends to show them. Instead, the photos would have to do, and she copied out the information she thought might be useful from the fragile pages.

In the *Courier*'s June 1951 issues came the first stirrings that the town might lose its rail service. The reporter cited the Maine Central Railroad's president, saying the company would cut back some of the short lines in a cost-cutting effort.

In the next week's Tuesday paper, an editorial caught her eye. Beverly had almost skipped over it, but the word "quarry" jumped out at her. The editor hinted broadly that business was not "as usual," nor "as it should be" at Burr Oak Quarry in Marble Cove.

She read on avidly, jotting down the gist of the editorial. From there onward, she read more closely, looking for mention of the limestone quarry in both the news columns and editorials. She also scanned the society and community pages in every issue. She amassed several pages of notes that she could share with her friends.

"Hello! Are you still up there?"

Beverly jumped and looked toward the stairs. She thought she recognized the voice of Gerald Kimball, the *Courier*'s reporter.

"Yes," she shouted. "Do I need to leave?"

Footsteps came slowly up the stairs. The tall man's head appeared first. He had lost most of his hair, but a stubborn tuft stuck up in the front. "Well, hello, Mayor." He stepped up into the attic.

Beverly smiled. "Hello, Gerald."

"Doing some research, I see."

"Yes, I was just reading up on the old quarry."

"Ah. Anything I should know about?"

"Not so far. If I find any hot tips, I'll let you know."

He smiled. "Why does the quarry interest you? Are you thinking it should be reopened?"

"Nothing like that." Beverly hesitated only a moment. Gerald Kimball possessed a wealth of knowledge about the town. "I'm actually interested in Elias Thorpe, the town's last stationmaster."

"Ah, the campaign to save the old depot."

"Yes, it's indirectly related to that. You see, I've been told Mr. Thorpe invested in the quarry."

"Is that right? Well, it might make a good nostalgia feature for the Saturday edition."

"I wouldn't mind a bit if you drew some attention to the depot," Beverly said. "Let me find out more about this business. If it looks like something that would interest your readers, I'll give you my notes. I'm writing down the date of each edition where I find anything relevant."

"Sounds good. Abby and I were going out to get a late lunch, and she remembered you had gone up here earlier. We didn't want to lock you in."

"Is it that late?" Beverly consulted her watch. "Goodness, I've been up here three hours!" She stood. "How time flies!

Is it all right if I leave these out? I'd like to come back another time and do some more reading."

"Of course," Gerald said. "Very few people come up here."

As she followed the reporter down the stairs, Beverly tried to plan another session in the archives. After she ate, she needed to work on her private clients' accounts. The regular council meeting was tonight. She sighed when they reached the ground floor.

Abby was waiting near the door. "Did you find what you needed, Mayor?"

"Yes, I found some interesting articles. I'd like to come back again soon, so I left some volumes out—but it may not be for a day or two."

"No problem," Abby said as they went outside.

Beverly said good-bye to the pair and went to her car. Her next headache would be apologizing to Mrs. Peabody for being late to lunch. And who had taken the puppy out? He didn't usually last this long during the daytime. She headed home prepared to meet disapproval, if not from her father, at least from Mrs. Peabody.

★ ★ ★

"We're going to make the raspberry sauce?" Margaret stared skeptically at Nicole. "I thought we could get it already made."

"The fresh sauce is what makes the raspberry trifle so flavorful," Nicole said. "Come on, it's not that hard. First you have to run the raspberries through the blender. Save a few out for your garnish, though."

"What about the seeds? I didn't think it had seeds in it."

"We'll sieve the pulp after you blend it."

"Oh." Margaret decided this dessert was a lot harder than Nicole had led her to believe. It had gone from "easy" to "not that hard." At least she was allowed to buy ladyfingers from the bakery. If she'd had to start those from scratch, she probably would have given up.

"Allan will love this," Nicole assured her.

"I hope so." Margaret bit her lip and followed instructions to a tee. An hour later, she and Nicole were looking at a truly elegant dessert in individual stemware dishes. The shaved chocolate and fresh berries atop the creamy mixture gave it class.

"I could eat the whole thing," Margaret said.

"You get to have a portion." Nicole got out two spoons and handed one to Margaret. They each picked up a dish and dug in.

"That is so good," Margaret said after her first bite. "I don't think I can do it alone, though."

"Of course you can. We made double the sauce, so you can take enough home with you and you won't have to make that part again tomorrow. Just follow the instructions for the rest, the way you did today."

"Can I call you tomorrow if something goes wrong?"

Nicole laughed. "I'll keep the hotline open, but it's going to be fine."

If only Margaret had her confidence.

"Now, let's go over your lists again," Nicole said. "First, the last-minute shopping list for the fresh things you'll need."

Margaret ticked off each item, and then got out her schedule for preparing the entire meal for Allan. Nicole talked her through it, describing how she would attack each step and make everything come out beautifully at the right time.

"I think you're ready to fly solo tomorrow." Nicole gave her a hug.

"How can I thank you enough?" Margaret asked.

"Take pictures. I want a photo of your table when it's ready."

"That's a great idea. And don't forget to come for your next painting lesson on Thursday."

Nicole smiled. "If my paintings start to turn out half as good as your dinner will be, I'll consider us more than even."

★ ★ ★

Beverly answered her phone just before supper, surprised to see that Diane was on the line.

"Hi! How are you, Diane?"

"I'm doing fine," her friend said. "Isn't tonight the town council meeting?"

"Yes, I'm heading over there at six thirty," Beverly said.

"How would you like some company?"

"You mean it?" Beverly asked. "You must be feeling well."

Diane chuckled. "I had a nap this afternoon, and I feel like getting out of the house tonight. You were so good to me yesterday, I thought maybe I could be the supportive one for you tonight."

"Thanks." Beverly sat back in her chair, smiling. "I'm never sure how many of the audience is in my corner at these meetings. It will be great to know at least one person is fully behind me."

The meeting went smoothly that evening, even though it included a discussion of the complaints about the snow plowing.

"This town has never paid for damaged mailboxes, and we never will, as long as I'm on the council," Jules Benton said.

"I understand your position, Mr. Benton," Beverly said. They'd had a private session earlier about that, and Mr. Benton firmly believed that once the town started paying for small property claims, they'd be nickel-and-dimed to death. "However, I would like it to go into the record that I have spoken to the road commissioner about the large number of complaints we had after the last storm. He has promised to go over a few points with all the plow drivers, and we all hope that this won't happen again, at least on this scale."

A smattering of applause greeted this statement, and Beverly suspected Diane led it. However, two residents got up and left the room with sour faces.

The budget was the next topic. To Beverly's surprise, treasurer Lionel Riley had ferreted out a few more places where they could trim the next year's expenses.

Councilwoman Martha Goodman, who favored economic development, had some suggestions for attracting more customers to the downtown merchants. Since most of the council members seemed to like her ideas, Beverly thanked her and asked if she would be willing to present them to the chamber of commerce. Martha readily agreed.

A few other small matters wrapped up the meeting. On the way to Diane's house, Beverly told her about the articles she had found in the *Courier* archives.

"Wonderful," Diane said. "Margaret and Shelley both think they could meet Thursday evening. Can you come? We'll gather at my house and talk all this over."

"Yes, I think so." Beverly stifled a yawn. "This day took the starch out of me."

"I'm a little tired, but not too much," Diane said. "Thanks for driving me. You did a terrific job tonight."

"Thank you. It was my pleasure to have your company." Beverly turned in at Diane's yard. "I'm glad you're doing so well."

Diane smiled. "This time the treatment wasn't nearly as bad as the last one, and really that one wasn't terrible. I'll see you soon." She got out of the car.

Beverly waited until Diane was inside and had turned off the porch light. She backed out of the drive and rolled up the street, thankful that this was home. She couldn't imagine going back to the big, empty house she used to occupy in Augusta.

"Hello," her father called as she went in the front door.

"Hi." While Beverly removed her boots, the curly gray puppy skittered out of the library and down the hall toward her. "Hello, little guy." She patted his head, a bit startled that she was smiling. She put away her boots and coat, shut the closet, and headed for the library. The puppy trotted along beside her.

"How did the meeting go?" her father asked.

Beverly sat down in the chair opposite him. "Quite well, thanks."

The puppy put his front paws up on her knee and looked up at her with a very human expression. She winced as a toenail scratched through her pant leg. When she carefully lifted his paw, he wriggled until somehow she'd lifted him onto her lap. He settled down on her knees, and she stroked his fluffy back. A pet's welcome could be comforting, she decided.

"You're warm," she said out loud.

"Careful," her father said. "You'll start to like him."

"No danger of that," she said amiably, while patting the puppy. The little pup nuzzled her hand, and Beverly laughed. "Well, not much."

CHAPTER TWENTY

The Wheeland house was quiet Wednesday morning. Mrs. Peabody would come in around eleven to fix lunch, but Beverly took advantage of the quiet hours between breakfast and her arrival to work in her upstairs office, putting together a budget analysis for her largest corporate client.

Her mind kept veering off to Jeff. He'd sent a short but rather stiff e-mail, telling her not to worry about their argument. *I'll get home tonight, and I'll try to come over tomorrow. We can talk it out then.*

She had written back, *Sounds good. I'll see you then.* All very practical and businesslike. But this was Jeff, the love of her life. Was this the most passion she could expect in the future? He certainly cared about the puppy. If he was this austere on an issue that meant so much to him, how would their married life go?

Pushing down her bleak thoughts, she forced herself to focus on the budget analysis. The complicated task absorbed all her attention for an hour, until a persistent yapping penetrated her concentration.

The puppy barked continuously. Beverly supposed her father had let him out into the back yard and now he wanted to come in. She listened for footsteps, but didn't hear any, and the barking sounded as if the pup was inside.

As she hesitated, a new sound came, and Beverly shivered. A high-pitched wail, the eerie whistle of a train, rang out distinctly.

She shoved her chair back and ran out into the hallway, her skin prickling with goose bumps.

"Father?" she called as she hurried to the top of the stairs.

At the bottom, the little gray puppy stood barking frantically. He gazed up at her with big brown eyes that seemed to plead with her to understand.

"What is it, boy?" Beverly dashed down the steps, and halfway there an acrid wave of smoke hit her.

★ ★ ★

The morning seemed to drag at the gallery. Margaret could hardly wait for Allan to arrive so that she could leave and get on with her plans. This time would be different from Valentine's Day—far different. This time, she would succeed.

Only two customers had come in by eleven o'clock, and neither of them made a purchase. Sometimes Margaret thought keeping the gallery open in winter wasn't really worth it. She should be working on her own painting. She'd neglected that lately.

After tonight, I'll get back to it, she promised herself. She needed to start a new batch of paintings for Matt

Beauregard's Lighting the Way greeting cards, and she needed to have several paintings in stock that she could display for sale when the summer traffic began.

She was too nervous this morning to get her paints out. She opened her laptop instead and checked her e-mail. She smiled at a message from her cousin Buddy.

Hey, Margaret! Are you getting cabin fever as bad as mine? I went ice fishing last week, but since we had that rain the ice is too soft now. Think we'll get an early spring?

She smiled at that and clicked Reply.

That would be nice! Now, you be careful—don't take any chances on the ice.

The next message was from one of the artists who exhibited in her gallery.

Margaret, just checking in. The check you sent for my painting that sold was most welcome. Should I do another for you? Dorothy

She typed back, *Absolutely! I still have one of yours on the wall, but I'd love to get a couple more before Memorial Day.*

She had already started work on an idea that would perhaps help both the gallery and the effort to save the railroad depot. Her next series of paintings would be of the old train station, as it had looked in its prime. Some nostalgia buff would surely be interested in them, but in the meantime, she would exhibit the paintings in the gallery's front window and draw attention to the station. People needed to realize how important the railroad had been to the town's economy in the past.

The bell over the front door jangled, and she hurried out into the main room of the gallery. The Reverend Silas Locke was coming in, looking around at the paintings on the walls.

"Hello, Reverend," Margaret said. He didn't come to the shop often. He was Beverly's pastor at Old First Church, and Margaret knew him fairly well.

"Good morning, Margaret," he said. "One of my parishioners tells me you've discovered a new artist who paints old sailing ships."

Margaret smiled. The reverend did have a few nautical prints hanging in his rather spartan home, she recalled. "Yes—that is, he's not new exactly, but his work is new to our gallery. His name is John Wyland, and he's very interested in historic ships. We have two on display, if you'd like to see them. Step right around to this section."

She led him around a divider, to where she'd hung Wyland's acrylics. One portrayed the *Red Jacket,* a famous clipper ship, and the *Snow Squall,* the last clipper built in Maine.

Reverend Locke studied the paintings for several minutes.

"I guess they're a little beyond my budget," he said at last, "but they're very interesting."

"They certainly are," Margaret said. "Part of Maine's heritage. You know, Mr. Wyland and I are talking about having some prints made of these. If he decides to go ahead with that, I'll let you know."

"Thank you," the reverend said.

Margaret thought she would not go amiss if she dropped his sister a note. Priscilla Abbott might appreciate knowing what her brother would like for his next birthday.

"What have you been up to?" the reverend asked.

"The usual," Margaret said.

"Have you and your friends taken up a new cause? We so much appreciate all you did to help restore Old First."

She smiled. "Thank you. We do have another interest. We'd like to see the old train station preserved. And, of course, we're trying to learn anything we can about Elias Thorpe."

"Hmm, yes. As I think I mentioned to you before, my family is distantly related, but I don't know much about him. I believe he left Marble Cove before I was born. We weren't closely related, but still, I always wondered what became of him."

"We'll keep you posted, and if you or Priscilla remembers anything about him, we'd love to hear it."

Silas frowned as though searching his memory. "You know, I do recall someone contacting my father once, when I was a teenager. They were trying to get in touch with Mr. Thorpe, but my father didn't know where he was at the time. I believe there was a general understanding that he had moved west."

"West?" Margaret asked. This was news, however vague.

"Yes—California, maybe, or Colorado. Somewhere out there." Silas shook his head. "Sorry, I don't remember anything definite. I don't know why this other person wanted to contact him, and I never heard that anyone tracked him down."

"He seems to have been an elusive character once he got on that train leaving Marble Cove."

Another customer came in, and the Reverend Locke took his leave. Margaret stayed fairly busy until Allan arrived to relieve her.

"How's business?" he called cheerfully as he entered.

"Not very good," Margaret admitted. "Half a dozen people have been in today, but no one seems to be buying."

"It's the end of February," Allan said with a shrug. "They're probably just making sure they haven't missed anything before the tourist season gears up again."

"Well, I hope you have a huge rush this afternoon, and they decide to buy whatever it is they like now." Margaret went to the back room to get her wraps and her purse.

Allan stood in the doorway watching her. "I hope you have a great afternoon."

She went over and put her hand up to his cheek. "I expect I will. And you'll close up at five and come straight home, right?"

"Whatever you want."

"That's what I want. Don't be late." She stood on tiptoe to kiss him.

★ ★ ★

"What is it, boy?" Beverly ran past the puppy into the kitchen.

Smoke poured from the top of the oven door. At once she knew what had happened. She had baked muffins at breakfast time and put the last pan in while she and her father had their second cup of coffee. Then she went upstairs and forgot about them.

She coughed and reached through the cloud of smoke to turn off the oven and switch on the fan above. Carefully she eased the oven door open a few inches, but a huge wave of smoke rolled out, and she could see the charred muffins in flames. She slammed the door shut. Probably her best course was to wait a while. She opened the back door and the window over the sink.

The puppy barked from the doorway. Beverly turned and scooped him up into her arms.

"You good boy!" How long would she have worked if he hadn't barked? It might have been some time before the smoke reached her in her office. And why hadn't the smoke alarm tripped? They would have to look into that as soon as the air cleared.

"What's going on? What's the dog so upset about?"

Beverly whirled toward the doorway. Her father stood there blinking, his face wrinkled in distaste.

"It's the muffins, but it's going to be all right. I'm so sorry. It's my fault. " She hurried to him and guided him down the hallway toward his library. The air was clearer here, but smoke hung like curtains near the ceiling.

"Open the front door too, and put on the bathroom fan," her father said.

"I will. Are you all right?"

"I'm fine," he said. "I must have dozed off, but when I woke up, Junior was barking and the house was full of smoke."

"Sit down." Beverly realized she still held the puppy. "Can you hold him? He's the one who alerted me, and I think we should be extranice to him today."

Her father sat in his recliner and held out his arms for the puppy. "Come here, boy."

"I can't believe I did that," Beverly said ruefully. "It was really stupid of me."

"Aw, don't beat yourself up over it." Her father stroked the puppy.

"I can't help it. I smelled the smoke, and I was terrified."

"It's all over now."

"Yes. But could you do me one favor?" she asked.

"What's that?"

"Stop calling that puppy 'Junior'!"

He laughed. "When you have a better name—"

"I'll think of one." She glared at him. "Jeff is coming tomorrow, and I will have a proper name for that dog."

"All right. But I'm warning you, I'll hold you to that."

Beverly huffed out a breath. She scurried around to open more windows, and the chill February air streamed through the house. They would burn some extra oil to bring the temperature back up later, but it would be worthwhile to get rid of the noxious smoke.

Her relief had solidified into anger at herself. How could she have been so careless?

"Hello?"

Mrs. Peabody came in the front door, looking about curiously.

"I'm in here, Mrs. Peabody." Beverly stepped out into the hall. "I'm sorry about this—I hoped to get the house aired out before you got here."

"What happened?"

"I did a very foolish thing." Beverly gave her a quick rundown of the scare. "Maybe you'd rather not go in the kitchen today— Oh! I forgot—the pan is still in the oven."

"I came to do a job, and it looks like you've got things under control." Mrs. Peabody started to take her coat off but shrugged back into it. "Maybe you can shut the doors now."

"Do you think so?" Beverly asked.

"It's freezing in here."

Meekly, Beverly went around to shut everything she'd just opened, but she left both fans going. When she went into the kitchen again, Mrs. Peabody was gingerly removing the blackened muffin tin from the oven.

"Let's just throw the whole thing out," Beverly said. "I don't think we could ever clean that up."

"I'm not one to be wasteful," the old woman said, "but in this case, I agree."

Beverly got out a fresh trash bag and had her toss the muffin pan into it. "I'll take this right out to the trash can, and then I'm going to take a look at that smoke detector. It should have gone off long before I discovered what was going on."

Mrs. Peabody didn't object, and a few minutes later Beverly got a folding step stool from the laundry room closet and climbed up to inspect the smoke alarm. When she removed the cover, the battery didn't look right to her. It seemed to be partway out of its slot and in danger of falling out.

She pushed it firmly back into place. A green light came on in the center of the unit. When she put the cover back in place, the light showed through.

"I guess that answers that. The battery wasn't installed correctly."

"Don't say anything to the mister," Mrs. Peabody said. "He might be upset if he was the last one to change it."

"He wasn't. I changed them all on New Year's Day." She walked to the stove and picked up the empty teakettle. "I think Father and I could use a cup of tea."

"I'll make it," Mrs. Peabody said. "You get that ladder out of the way."

"Thanks." Beverly collapsed the step stool and took it back to the laundry room. When she returned to the kitchen, Mrs. Peabody had the teakettle heating and was setting the teapot and mugs on a tray.

"Do you want anything to eat with that?"

"No, thank you. Wouldn't want to spoil our dinner. But I will take a treat for the puppy." Beverly got one of the small dog biscuits she'd bought at the pet store and placed it on a saucer.

When the tea was ready, she carried the tray to the library. Her father sat in his customary chair, with the puppy on his lap, browsing a magazine. Beverly poured out his tea and set the mug on a coaster near him.

"And as for you, young fellow," she said, holding eye contact with the puppy, "here is your treat." She set the saucer on the floor, and the pup jumped down from her father's lap and snatched the biscuit.

Beverly sat down and took her own tea mug. "I checked the smoke detector in the kitchen. The battery wasn't in right."

"Oh?" Her father arched his eyebrows.

"It's all my fault—that and leaving the muffins in the oven." Beverly shook her head. "I should have tested that alarm last month, after I changed the battery. If the puppy hadn't barked so furiously, I might not have noticed the smoke for a while. We could have had much worse results to deal with."

"Well, don't fret about it," her father said. "We all make mistakes. I know I forget things. And you've been very busy lately."

"That's no excuse. But you can be sure I'll be more careful from now on," Beverly said.

The puppy finished crunching his biscuit and looked up at her quizzically. Just in time she realized what he intended and set down her hot mug. The pup jumped up into her lap. She and her father both laughed, and Beverly patted him. She tried not to mind his toenails as he shifted about and settled in a comfortable position on her knees.

"Looks like you've got a friend now," her father said.

"I think I can stand it." She held the puppy's head and scratched under his chin. "I may even bring you an extraspecial treat later."

And she *would* find a name for the brave little puppy.

★ ★ ★

Margaret fluttered around the kitchen, consulting her list, taking items from the refrigerator, and tending one of the dishes on the counter. Meanwhile, Adelaide put her finishing touches on the table.

"Look, Mom! See how pretty the placemats look."

Margaret walked over and gazed at the pink paper mats her daughter had made. "They're beautiful, honey. I especially love the hearts on the edges."

"Penny showed me how to cut them out right. It's easy if you know how."

Margaret smiled. "Someday you'll have to show me."

"I told her this was supposed to be for Valentine's Day, and she thought it would look nice."

"Well, I love it."

Lights swept across the wall, heralding the arrival of a car in the driveway. Margaret looked out the window. "Oh, Mrs. Kling is here for you."

Adelaide's mouth opened in surprise. "Dad's not home yet."

"It's all right. You've finished with the table, and it looks great. Get your coat." Margaret took a quick look around the kitchen to make sure she could leave it for a moment without a disaster striking. She went into the living room with Adelaide and opened the door.

Maryann Kling stood on the porch. "Hi, Mrs. Hoskins. My mom's in the car."

"Hello, Maryann," Margaret said. "I hope you girls have a good time tonight."

"We will."

"I'm ready!" Adelaide hurried over, pulling on her striped scarf.

"Don't forget your tote bag," Margaret said.

"Oh yeah. The game is in there." Adelaide dashed back to the couch and scooped up her tote. "See you later, Mom."

Margaret pecked her on the cheek, and they were out the door. She waved to Elsa Kling, who returned her wave from behind the wheel of her minivan.

As soon as they moved out of the driveway, Margaret shut the door and hurried back to the kitchen. She checked the oven, where the chicken was starting to brown. The clock showed five after five. She put ice in the water glasses and took the plastic wrap off the plate of appetizers. The meatballs simmered in the slow cooker.

As if on cue, another car pulled in. Margaret made herself breathe slowly. Should she take the salad out now, or wait? She grabbed her master schedule off the counter.

"Hey," Allan called as he came through the front door. "Something smells good in here. Margaret?"

"In the kitchen."

He came to the doorway and glanced at the table. "What's this?"

She went over to kiss him. "Are you really surprised?"

"I really am. I knew something was going on, but I had no idea what."

"None at all?" She found that hard to believe.

"Well, maybe just a teeny-tiny inkling. But it might just as easily have been a new painting."

"Sure. Welcome to Margaret's Gourmet Restaurant. And this time, I hope it's edible."

He put his arms around her. "I can hardly wait."

* * *

"Beverly, Jeff's here!"

As if she didn't already know that. Up in her bedroom, Beverly patted a stray hair into place and laid down her brush. She turned to the bed.

"Are you ready?" She slapped her hand on her thigh, and the puppy barked. He wriggled to the edge of the bed and hopped down. "Come on, you." Beverly lifted him and carried him out into the hallway.

At the bottom of the stairs, Jeff was handing his coat to her father. He looked up at her warily.

"Hey."

"Hi." Beverly smiled and descended slowly, holding the puppy so that he faced Jeff.

"Is he climbing stairs now? I hope he wasn't naughty to go up there," Jeff said anxiously.

"No, I took him up."

Jeff's eyebrows shot up. "Really?" He glanced at her father.

"They've made their peace," Father said. "As should the two of you. Go on into the living room. I'll put some coffee on."

"All right," Beverly said, "but when it's ready you let me get the tray."

"Don't worry, I will." He ambled off to the kitchen.

In the living room, Beverly sat down on the sofa and held the puppy. Jeff sat gingerly next to her, almost as if he was ready to jump up if she said the wrong thing. The pup wiggled and whined.

"He wants to come see you," Beverly said.

"Okay." Jeff smiled then and reached out to pat the puppy. "Hi, buddy. Do you remember me?"

Beverly released her grip, and the puppy bounded into Jeff's lap. Jeff chuckled and stroked him, and the pup bobbed up to lick his face.

"You're not mad anymore?"

Beverly shook her head. "Wait until you hear what he did yesterday. He's part of the family now. And I'm really sorry that I made you feel bad."

Jeff frowned and gave a little shrug. "You were right. I shouldn't have given you an animal without asking first. They require a lot of care."

"I've come to terms with it. Father and I both think Scamp is worth the bother."

"Scamp?" Jeff asked.

"That's right, unless you hate it. Shelley called him that a couple of weeks ago, and I think it fits."

Jeff patted the puppy, looking him over, and nodded. "I can see that."

"Thank you. Because Father's default name for him was 'Junior,' and I hated it."

Jeff laughed. "So what happened yesterday?"

"He saved my father's life."

Jeff's hands stilled. "Are you serious?"

"Maybe that's a little melodramatic, but I'd left some muffins in the oven and they burned up. The smoke detector didn't go off, and by the time I realized something was wrong, the downstairs was full of smoke. If Scamp hadn't kept barking until I checked—well, I know I could have gotten out all right if I'd needed to, but I'm not so sure about Father. The food was actually in flames, Jeff. And that puppy was protecting us."

"Wow. But you're all okay?"

"Yes. I doubt the fire would have spread, but I've been thinking about what smoke inhalation could have done to my father, and let me tell you, this little guy is a hero."

"So...you're sure you want to keep him?"

"Absolutely. Don't even think of taking him away from here."

Jeff slid his arm around her and pulled her closer, with the puppy between them. "Thank you. I love you so much."

Tears filled Beverly's eyes. "I know. And I know you would have found him a new home if I couldn't deal with it. But God intervened. It wasn't just the oven fire. There were other things, before that. Did you know some dogs are afraid of thunderstorms?"

"Well, sure. I mean, I know *people* who are scared of them. Why wouldn't a little puppy be afraid?"

"This one is. He needs comfort sometimes."

"I think we can handle it between the two of us."

"So do I," Beverly said.

"And after we're married, I'll do all the parts that aren't fun. I'll take him out when it's rainy, and if he's sick, I'll clean up after him."

She laughed. "I know that too. You love that mutt so much!"

"I wish I could keep him until the wedding," Jeff said.

"Oh no you don't. He's staying right here. But you come visit him lots, won't you?"

"Gladly. I'm so proud of you. Thank you for sticking it out, and for appreciating him." Jeff leaned over to kiss her.

Just three more months, Beverly thought. *Three more months until the wedding.*

"*Ahem.*"

She opened her eyes, and Jeff pulled away from her.

"Sorry," her father said. "The coffee's ready."

* * *

That evening, Diane hosted a gathering of the four friends. It seemed to her a long time since they had all been together. Shelley brought a plate of mixed pastries, and Diane brewed oolong tea and decaffeinated coffee.

"It's so good to have you all here," she told them when all were seated in her living room near the stone fireplace. She looked from face to face, silently thanking God for these dear friends, this wonderful family she had found in Marble Cove. A blaze crackled merrily and warmed them as they enjoyed their refreshments in companionable quiet for a moment.

"Are you feeling well, Diane?" Shelley asked.

"Yes, I am, thanks." Diane got up and took a card from the mantel. "Let me show you all this. It came this morning, from Jessica's fiancé." She read his message once again: *"Mom," thank you so much for your encouragement. I'm learning your daughter is just as strong and supportive as you are. I'm so proud to be joining your family! Love, Martin*

She handed the card to Margaret, who read it silently.

"Oh, that's so sweet. He's definitely a keeper." Margaret passed the card to Beverly.

"That's great," Beverly said, passing the card to Shelley.

"And how are things with Leo?" Shelley asked.

"Not bad. We're going to go out soon."

"Really?" Margaret asked. "That's wonderful. At least, I think it is."

Diane sat down between her and Beverly, smiling. "Yes, I think so. I'm ready to explore the possibility of romance again."

"Hooray," Shelley said. "I'm rooting for Leo, but if he's not the one, at least you're ready for something new."

Beverly just gave her a smile, but Diane knew her friend was behind her.

"If it's something new you want, you can still try ballroom dancing with Allan and me," Margaret said.

Diane chuckled. "I'll let you know. Margaret, wasn't last night your big surprise for Allan?"

"Yes, it was, and everything went beautifully this time."

Margaret was so obviously pleased with the outcome that they all expressed their approval.

"It was the first time in my life that I prepared a meal with more than two dishes that were all ready to eat at the same time." They all laughed, and Margaret's face took on a wistfulness. "You know, the best moment was when he tasted the chicken, and his face lit up. I could tell he was proud of me."

"Congratulations," Diane said.

"It was a milestone," Margaret admitted. "And I'm happy to know I'm still capable of learning new things."

Shelley leaned forward and focused on Beverly. "Hey, didn't I see Jeff's SUV in your driveway this afternoon?"

Beverly took a quick sip of her tea and nodded. "That's right. He didn't stay long, but we had a good visit."

Diane remembered her friend's confession of the argument she'd had with Jeff about the puppy.

Beverly smiled at her, as if reading her thoughts. "We agree at last about the puppy's future."

"Is Jeff going to give him to someone else?" Diane asked.

"Not at all. In fact, I've changed my position on that. You'll all probably be happy to know that I now believe Scamp is a good addition to the family."

"Scamp!" Shelley clapped her hands together.

Beverly smiled at her. "You came up with that name."

"It fits him perfectly," Diane said. "But what happened to make you change your mind? Other than his being an adorable little sweetheart, I mean."

Beverly filled them in on the puppy's bravery, and they all agreed that he had earned his place in the household.

"There was one thing I didn't tell anyone else about," Beverly said thoughtfully. "Right at first, when Scamp started barking, but before I smelled the smoke, I thought I heard a train whistle."

They all fell silent.

"I was going to ask Father if he heard it, but he didn't even hear Scamp barking—he'd dozed off in his chair, and that's what really scared me. He might never have woken up if he'd been there alone and the smoke got worse. But that told me the situation was serious. In fact, it scared me."

"Understandably," Margaret said.

Diane added, "One more thing to be thankful for."

After a moment's silence, Shelley said, "Your father might even want to get a dog of his own, after you move out and take Scamp with you."

Beverly chuckled. "I wouldn't go that far."

Diane rose. "Let me refill everyone's cups, and then I'd like Beverly to share what she learned at the *Courier* archives this week. She found quite a bit about the old quarry, and some intriguing bits about Elias Thorpe."

Beverly opened her notebook and went through the items she had jotted down about the old stationmaster—more about his lavish parties, his investment in the Burr Oak Quarry, and of course his mysterious disappearance.

"The *Courier* did several pieces about the upcoming end of rail service to Marble Cove in early 1952," she said. "After the quarry closed, there wasn't enough freight business to keep the line profitable. The railroad came in and told the town officials they just couldn't keep running trains down here. And then the scandal broke. I'm surprised Augie didn't mention it when we talked to him a few months back, but maybe it slipped his mind."

"A scandal? So now we get to the good part," Shelley said.

Beverly smiled. "It depends on how you look at it. It seems that at a town council meeting three weeks before the last train rolled out of here, one of the council members stood up and accused several of the quarry's investors of skimming profits from the business. He said that led to the quarry's closing, and it hurt a lot of people in the town— those who worked at the quarry, those who depended on the trains, and those who had invested in good faith."

"Let me guess," Diane said. "Elias Thorpe was one of those accused of skimming."

Beverly nodded. "Afraid so. And three weeks later, he boarded the last train out of town and vanished."

Margaret looked around at the others. "Well, we've made some progress and uncovered some interesting history, if nothing else."

"Yes," Diane said, "but will it be enough to save the old train station?"

About the Author

Susan Page Davis is the author of more than forty published novels. A Maine native, she now lives in western Kentucky with her husband Jim. They have six children and eight grandchildren. Susan is a past winner of the Carol Award and the Inspirational Readers' Choice Award, as well as Heartsong Presents Favorite Author of the Year. Her novel *Captive Trail* won the 2012 Will Rogers Medallion for Western fiction.

A CONVERSATION WITH
SUSAN PAGE DAVIS

Q. This is your third book in Miracles of Marble Cove. What has been the most rewarding aspect of writing for this series? The most challenging?

A. The most rewarding has been hearing readers' reactions to the stories. It's wonderful to be part of a series like this that touches people's hearts. The most challenging for me in this book was dealing with Diane's cancer, as my mom and dad both went through that. I know a lot of our readers either had, have, or know someone with cancer, and I hope they'll find Diane's struggle uplifting.

Q. Other than the four main characters in the series, which character have you enjoyed writing about most?

A. I like Jeff a lot. He's sort of a maverick, and in this book he caused a little trouble. Working things out with him, Beverly, and Scamp was fun.

Q. Each of the four women has started a new career in the course of the series. If you were to try a new career right now, what would you like to do?

A. Since I love research, I might try something that involves that, like being a professional genealogist. I adore finding those fascinating nuggets in musty old tomes.

Q. Other than your writing for Miracles of Marble Cone, what is your favorite fiction genre to write, and why?

A. I have written quite a few historical romances, and I enjoy that. Most of them also have some aspect of mystery in them. I love doing the research and learning about old customs and cultures. I'm glad I have my modern conveniences, but I love being transported back in time with a good historical novel, for a few hours of enjoyment.

BAKING WITH SHELLEY

Grandma Bauer's Depression-Era Cake

This cake was popular during the Great Depression because it didn't require eggs, butter, or milk.

1 cup brown sugar, firmly packed
1½ cups water
⅓ cup vegetable oil
2 cups dark raisins
2 teaspoons cinnamon
½ teaspoon ground cloves
½ teaspoon ground nutmeg
1 teaspoon baking soda
1 teaspoon salt
2 teaspoons water
2 cups flour
1 teaspoon baking powder

Preheat oven to 325 degrees. Combine sugar, water, oil, raisins, and spices in a saucepan, and boil for three minutes, stirring frequently. Take pan off heat and let cool for ten minutes.

Dissolve baking soda and salt in two teaspoons of water and add to raisin mixture (it will foam). Blend in the flour and baking powder. Mix well. Pour batter into a greased nine-inch-square pan, and bake for fifty-five minutes or until toothpick inserted in center comes out clean. Let cake cool for about ten minutes before serving. Serves ten to twelve.

From the
Guideposts Archives

This story by Helen S. McCutcheon of
Lakeland, Florida, originally appeared in the
January 1987 issue of *Guideposts*.

It was 5:30 PM when my three children and I left the
grocery store, so in order to be home before dark, we took
the shortcut. A cold mist fell—the dreariness of a February
dusk in Michigan. When we came to the train tracks, my six-
year-old, Lynda, tripped and fell, and her right foot became
wedged between the wooden tie and the steel track.

"Untie your shoe, honey, and slip your foot out," I said.
But Lynda had already pulled her shoelace into a tight
knot. I tried to unravel the knot with my house key, then a
hairpin. Still it held fast. I tried yanking Lynda's foot free
of the shoe, but it wouldn't come. I had to get the knot
untied.

Starting to worry, I scooted my other two children down
the embankment, then dropped my bag of groceries and ran
back to Lynda.

Just then I felt a faint vibration. An approaching train! I dug at the knot—ripping my nails, bloodying my fingers. Lynda and I both broke into fearful sobbing.

"Oh, God," I cried, "Help us. Please, God."

Two little faces stared up at me from the ditch, terror-stricken. My eyes then strayed to the spilled bag of groceries.

"The ham! The ham!" I screamed in a strange fit of revelation. I grabbed the canned ham, ripped the key from its bottom and peeled off the lid. Using the sharp edge of the lid, I severed the shoelace and pulled Lynda out of her shoe. In the glare and roar of the oncoming train we tumbled into the ditch. Safe.

Now, I've heard it said that God gives us what we need when we need it. But I've since wondered, *What did the Lord give me just then? The sharp lid on a can of ham or an imagination sharpened to the quick?*

Read on for a sneak peek of the next exciting book in
Miracles of Marble Cove!

Tracks and Ties
by Camy Tang

S helley Bauer hummed as she finished piping the icing onto another batch of chocolate whoopee pie halves. The fat dollops of mint-green buttercream made her want to scoop some out with her finger like a kid.

She restrained herself and carefully picked up an unfrosted half and began to top each whoopee pie, going down the row on her cooling rack.

A knock at the door was followed by a tentative "Shelley?"

"Hi, Beverly!" Shelley called. "Come on in! I'm in the kitchen."

Shelley gestured to two other rows of cooling racks with cakelike chocolate cookies lying in wait to be frosted and assembled. "I'm making whoopee pies. Would you like a taste?"

"They look delicious," Beverly said, "but I came over to give you this." She laid a manila folder on the table, away from the assembled whoopee pies already stacked there. "It's a form for you to fill out that will make it easier for you to prepare your taxes."

"Thanks, Beverly. That'll help a lot." Now that Shelley owned a moderately successful business, the Bauers' yearly tax returns had gotten much more complicated.

There was another knock at the door, which immediately opened with a "*Yoo hoo!* Hello, Shelley!"

"Hi, Margaret! Come on in!" Shelley called, and was surprised to hear Aiden run from the living room to greet not only Margaret but Diane as well.

"I guess both Margaret and Diane are here," Beverly said from where she sat at the kitchen table.

"I hope it's not bad news or anything like that." Shelley finished icing the last whoopee pie on the second rack and began setting the other chocolate halves on top of the mint buttercream mounds.

Soon both Margaret and Diane entered the kitchen. "Hello!" Diane said. "We saw Beverly heading over to your house."

"And, naturally, we wanted to make sure we got in on any treats that might be available for tasting." Margaret winked.

Shelley giggled. "I'm afraid these whoopee pies are spoken for. Wanda Bacon—Aiden's Sunday school teacher—is throwing a birthday party tonight for her husband, and she hired me to make these whoopee pies. Mint chocolate is his favorite."

Margaret looked longingly at one on the table. "Mint chocolate is my favorite too."

Diane nudged her in the ribs. "Since when?"

"Since right now."

Shelley rolled her eyes. "Lucky for you I just happen to have some rejects from this batch that I'm happy to let you sample."

"Lucky us, indeed." Margaret sat down at the kitchen table with an eager smile.

"Can I help?" Diane asked.

"Did you want to pour some coffee for all of us? I think there's enough for everyone in the pot I made earlier." Shelley concentrated on frosting the last rack of whoopee pies.

"How is your writing coming along?" Margaret asked Diane as she began pouring mugs of coffee.

"My novel is moving along at a good pace," Diane said.

"And your devotional book?" Beverly licked frosting off her finger.

"It's turning out to be more of a challenge than I had thought it would be," Diane said, "because it's so…personal."

"That's understandable," Margaret said. "But I'm sure that sharing your heart and your experiences will be a huge encouragement to your readers."

"What's been encouraging to me is reading through the entries again," Diane said. "I had forgotten some of the things I'd written, and reading them reminded me to trust in God and be grateful for the good things He's given me. Like all of you." Diane smiled at them all and then turned thoughtful. "Going through cancer a second time has really helped me remember that friendships are precious. I want to do all I can to keep the ones I have strong and healthy, and repair any that need nurturing."

Shelley and Margaret smiled back at Diane, but Beverly seemed pensive. "That's good advice for me, especially in light of what I've been thinking about today," she said.

"Oh?" Shelley asked. "I hope there haven't been any wedding disasters." It had only been a few years since her own wedding, and she vividly recalled so many things that almost went wrong at the last minute.

"Oh no. Not disasters," Beverly said. "I want to ask my cousin Charlotte to be a bridesmaid, but we had a falling-out when I married Will and our relationship has never been the same since." Beverly had already told Shelley and Margaret that she'd asked Diane to be her matron of honor, and they'd been supportive of her since they knew she and Diane had a special bond.

"Charlotte?" Diane leaned forward on her elbows on Shelley's kitchen table. "I don't think you've ever mentioned her."

"She's a cousin from my mom's side. We were very close growing up, but we drifted apart when I married Will."

"Did you both just get too busy?" Margaret asked.

Beverly swallowed. "I wish that was the case. I sort of gave in to pressure from Will to choose my attendants from his family and friends." Beverly looked up at her friends to see their reaction before continuing. "Charlotte was very hurt by that decision, and I felt terrible about it later."

"Maybe enough time has passed, and she'll be willing to listen and forgive," Shelley said.

Beverly nodded. "I hope so. I really do want Charlotte in my bridal party now."

"We'll be praying that she's open to talking to you," Diane said.

"Thanks. That makes me feel a lot better."

Shelley turned to Margaret. "How's your painting going?"

Margaret smiled, although her eyes didn't brighten. "Oh, it's fine."

She didn't look fine at all. Shelley said hesitatingly, "Are you sure? I don't mean to pry..."

Margaret sighed. "Oh, you're not prying. I'm just a little blue from the weather, that's all. I get that way a lot in the early springtime because I'm tired of the snow and the cold."

"I think if you look around, you could be inspired, even by the winter landscape," Diane noted.

"You mean by the slush and ice and sleet?" Margaret asked.

"Well, no. By how the trees look in March—not leafy like they are in the summertime, but stark and black and softened with snow," Diane said.

"Or how the ocean always looks darker in wintertime," Shelley said.

"You started that beautiful painting of the train depot," Beverly said. "Could you make it a series?"

Margaret's expression had changed from dejected to thoughtful. She gave them all a warm smile. "That's a good idea. I don't have anything to lose and it might be just what I need to get out of this funk."

"Oh!" Shelley straightened and eyed the clock. "I'm sorry to chase you all out, but I need to leave soon to deliver these whoopee pies to Wanda."

Beverly glanced at her watch. "I need to get home to cook dinner for Father."

"And I need to take Rocky for a walk." Diane rose to her feet.

After her three friends returned to their own homes, Shelley packed up the treats and then looked in on Dan and the kids playing Candy Land. They radiated love and happiness, and Shelley sent up a prayer of thanks at how God had blessed her and her family.

"Sorry to interrupt your game," Shelley said, "but I'm heading out to deliver the whoopee pies."

"No problem." Dan flashed her a smile. "I'll still be winning when you get back."

"Uncle Dan!" Hailey protested, and Aiden said, "I can beat you, Daddy!" Emma joined in with their laughter.

Shelley packed the boxes of desserts in her car and headed out. As she approached the Victorian houses along Sullivan Street, she noticed how the lights in the windows shone cheerfully against the twilight. She drove slowly, peering at house numbers so she wouldn't miss Wanda's house. She'd known Wanda for years through church but had never been to her home.

Shelley suddenly stopped short as a familiar house came into view. The darkness pulled away from a pale blue Victorian sitting back from the street.

At first, Shelley didn't know why the house was so familiar, and why it struck her in such a strange way. Then it hit her—this was Elias Thorpe's old house, and the reason it looked so odd was because there were lights on inside.

Shelley squinted but couldn't see through the windows. She had thought the owners were still wintering in Florida and weren't expected back until later this spring.

Shelley continued on toward Wanda's house and found it easily. She pulled up behind two vans parked in the driveway, grabbed the boxes of whoopee pies, and headed up the cement walkway to the front door.

One side of the white double doors opened immediately when she rang the doorbell, and over the muted cacophony of enthusiastic conversations emanating from the depths of the house, Wanda greeted her. "Hi, Shelley! You're right on time. Come on in while I set these down and get my checkbook."

Shelley entered the spacious foyer and closed the door behind her. The warm smell of dinner reached her nose while the noise of the partyers echoed off the white walls. Shelley waited, looking at the porcelain figurines in a glass display case against one wall.

Wanda returned in a few seconds, holding a blue leather checkbook. "How much do I owe you?"

Shelley told her, and Wanda bent over a mahogany side table and wrote out a check to her.

"Sounds like quite a party," Shelley said.

Wanda rolled her eyes as she handed Shelley the check. "You wouldn't believe. I'm sure they can hear us all the way down the street."

"Actually, I noticed that there were lights on at the Inglewoods' house down the street. Aren't they away in Florida for the winter?"

Wanda's face suddenly became a polite mask. "Oh, don't worry," she said casually. "They came back early this year."

"Oh. That's good. My friends and I will be able to visit them this coming week to chat with them."

A strange look passed briefly over Wanda's face. She opened her mouth as if to say something, but then changed her mind and closed it.

"What is it?" Shelley asked.

"Oh, nothing." Wanda gave a stiff smile.

Wanda had been acting strangely ever since Shelley mentioned the owners of the former Thorpe house. "Do you know the owners very well?"

"No, they don't really talk to us." Wanda's voice had a hint of tightness, and Shelley was surprised because Wanda was such a friendly person. She couldn't imagine Wanda not being on cordial terms with any of her neighbors.

"Are they just not very talkative?" Shelley asked.

"You could say that," Wanda said, her tone dry. "If you do go speak to them about their house, I'm not sure how chatty they'll be. They like to keep to themselves quite a bit."

Shelley got the impression that Wanda was understating the situation and too polite to say more. She knew she wouldn't get anything more out of Wanda, whom she'd never known to speak a bad word about anyone.

"Well, thanks for letting me know." Shelley headed to the door. "Enjoy your party."

"Thanks for the whoopee pies." Wanda held the door open for Shelley. "I'm sure my husband will love them."

As Shelley drove home, she slowed again in front of Elias Thorpe's old house. Shelley was excited to find out the Inglewoods were indeed home, and she couldn't wait to tell her friends so they could plan to visit them. But Wanda's demeanor made her wary.

A momentary chill passed over Shelley. What secrets might still be hidden in the old Thorpe house? And what did the Inglewoods know about the mysterious man who had owned the home before them?

A NOTE FROM THE EDITORS

We hope you enjoyed Miracles of Marble Cove, published by the Books and Inspirational Media Division of Guideposts, a nonprofit organization that touches millions of lives every day through products and services that inspire, encourage, help you grow in your faith, and celebrate God's love.

Thank you for making a difference with your purchase of this book, which helps fund our many outreach programs to military personnel, prisons, hospitals, nursing homes, and educational institutions.

We also create many useful and uplifting online resources. Visit Guideposts.org to read true stories of hope and inspiration, access OurPrayer network, sign up for free newsletters, download free e-books, join our Facebook community, and follow our stimulating blogs.

To learn about other Guideposts publications, including the best-selling devotional *Daily Guideposts*, go to Guideposts .org/Shop, call (800) 932-2145, or write to Guideposts, PO Box 5815, Harlan, Iowa 51593.